"LAST TIME, you went into the Greek myth when you touched the scan of that gold pendant of Dionysus, the Greek god. And when you touched the same thing on the other side, you came back," Cleo told her brother.

"Yeah, I was there. I got that," Alex said.

"So get this." Cleo pulled a plastic bag from her lap and dropped the fragment of the stone bowl into it. "Take this with you. Anything over there gets too hairy, you just reach in, touch this, and zip, you're home. Do not pass Go, do not collect two hundred dollars."

Alex hesitated. But really, there was nothing else to be done. Their father was gone, and this was their only lead. He nodded and took the plastic bag back from his sister.

Turning, Alex stood before the plasma screen. He reached out to the three-dimensional image of the snake bowl and touched it. There was a flash of light and Alex Bellows was gone . . .

. . . and the bowl fragment inside the plastic bag dropped to the ground.

Cleo watched the bag fall to the floor and her eyes opened wide in fear. The fragment hadn't gone through. Her plan had failed. Whatever mystical power opened the gateway to the Alterworld, it would not send any objects through, only people. Which meant Alex was trapped. Again.

BOOK II

Hammer of the Gods

A novelization by
John Whitman

BASED ON THE TELEPLAY BY GILLIAN HORVATH

BANTAM BOOKS
New York · Toronto · London · Sydney · Auckland

RL 5.5, AGES 10 and up
HAMMER OF THE GODS
A Bantam Skylark Book / January 2003

ISBN: 0-553-48760-4 (pbk.)
0-553-13018-8 (lib. bdg.)

Visit us on the Web! www.randomhouse.com/kids
Educators and librarians, for a variety of teaching tools,
visit us at www.randomhouse.com/teachers

Published simultaneously in the United States and Canada

Bantam Skylark is an imprint of Random House Children's
Books, a division of Random House, Inc. SKYLARK BOOK
and colophon and BANTAM BOOKS and colophon are
registered trademarks of Random House, Inc. Bantam Books,
1540 Broadway, New York, New York 10036.

PRINTED IN THE UNITED STATES OF AMERICA
OPM 10 9 8 7 6 5 4 3 2 1

MythQuest

Book II

Hammer of the Gods

Chapter One

His name was Loki, and he was a god. He was known as the breaker of boundaries, the bringer of mischief. He had sharp eyes and an even sharper tongue, and not a single person, god or mortal, wanted to be on the wrong end of his razor-edged wit. He could steal a glance, steal a scene, and then steal away without being caught. Some said he was a god of fire, since he was the brightest of the Norse gods. Others claimed his name meant "spider," because he could spin a web of lies when he wanted to. He was the maker of the first net that had ever been created.

But he had been snared.

Loki, the trickster, had run out of tricks. He stood now on a strip of barren ground somewhere near the edge of Asgard, the home of the Norse gods. For the first time in all the ages, Loki actually felt small. The other Norse gods had always been bigger than he was, but that had never seemed to matter before, when he had walked among them, joking with and mocking them. Now they seemed to tower over him, glaring down at him as he stood in the center of their circle. The most frightening of them all was Thor, the god of thunder and lightning, Loki's onetime friend.

"Do you have anything to say for yourself, Loki?" Thor demanded, scowling down at Loki, his mouth hard beneath his thick blond beard.

Loki looked at Thor's angry face and then let his gaze wander around the circle.

Thor's wife, Sif, stood at her husband's side, her hair of spun gold, shining. Next, dressed all in white, was Heimdall, the guardian of the Norse gods. Heimdall, it was said, had ears so keen he could hear the grass grow, and eyes so sharp he could see for a hundred miles by night or day. Loki felt those eyes on him now and shuddered.

Next to Heimdall stood Freya, goddess of love, wearing her magical cloak of birds' feathers and a beautiful necklace.

Loki's eyes fell on a scowling god with a gray beard and a patch over one eye: Odin, father of the gods. Odin was the all-powerful ruler of their world, and he gave Loki such a dark, hateful look that Loki had to turn away.

Hoping to find a friendlier face, Loki turned to his own family. His wife, Sigyn, stood nearby. She was loyal to him, but he could find no comfort in her presence, for she could not help him here. Beside her stood their two sons, Vali and Narvi, handsome boys who looked far more heroic than their clever father. But, Loki told himself, they lacked his cleverness, his ability to defy the laws of the other gods. They followed rules instead of breaking them, and that disappointed him. Of course, it occurred to him that if he'd spent less time running around breaking rules himself, he might have been able to teach them better.

Finally, he turned back to Thor. He felt a

twinge of fear as he stared up at the mass of muscle. Physically, Thor could crush him like a bug. But when it came to brains, Thor was a dwarf and Loki was a giant. He felt the fear drain away as he said, "What, you speak for Odin the Allfather now, Thor? Or is Odin now father of nothing?"

Thor's face turned red. "Odin is father of Balder!"

"Whom you killed!" yelled another goddess, named Frigga. "Odin feels too much sorrow to speak!"

Loki winced. Frigga was Odin's wife and the mother of Balder, the god they were accusing him of killing. Then, inwardly, Loki grinned. If you looked at it one way, he thought, he *had* murdered that sickly sweet Balder. But Loki never looked at things in a way that made him guilty. Why bother?

"I didn't kill your son, Frigga," he said out loud. "I just happened to be there when it happened."

Frigga, though, wasn't afraid of the crafty little god. "You're a liar, Loki!"

Thor stepped forward. "Loki, we all know your tricks. You are responsible for what happened."

Loki shrugged. "You're angry because Balder is dead, but I don't see one of you here who's any better than I am. You were all trying to kill him!"

Thor scoffed. "That was only a game!"

Loki yawned. "It's always just a game."

Thor raised a clenched fist. "You made the spear that killed him."

Loki's eyes twinkled. "Ah, but I didn't use it, did I?"

For a brief instant Loki thought he'd scored a point, but when he saw the dark look of the brooding god, he suddenly realized that this wasn't a game after all.

Chapter Two

Alex Bellows was chugging milk from the carton when the doorbell rang. Still holding the carton, he strolled down the hall, hearing his footsteps echo in the house. Sometimes, with his father gone, the place felt very empty. It was on afternoons like this that his dad would have been working up in the computer room. Dr. Matt Bellows had spent his life studying ancient myths and legends and collecting ancient artifacts that depicted them. In the last few years, he'd helped develop a computer program that created three-dimensional images of these artifacts so he could study them even when he didn't have the priceless objects in his possession. But Dr. Bellows had disappeared weeks earlier, and no one knew where to look for him.

Well, almost no one.

Alex and his sister, Cleo, had discovered a clue. More than a clue, really—an enormous secret. They had discovered a way to enter the three-dimensional holographs their father had created. They could actually go into the imaginary worlds described by the ancient myths. It should have been impossible, of course. Alex had actually done it, and even *he* found it hard to believe. Traveling back in time might have been a little easier to swallow. But this wasn't time travel—he didn't go to places that had ever existed. Just places of myths and legends. Alex and Cleo were convinced that their father had somehow become lost somewhere among these ancient artifacts of the world.

Alex reached the front door and opened it to find his father's colleague, Barbara Frazier, standing there. She wore a stiff smile that didn't seem to fit her face. It made him think of a mask or a fake mustache that was about to fall off.

"Hello, Alex," Barbara Frazier said. "Can I come in?"

Alex hesitated. Dr. Frazier hadn't exactly been their best friend since his father disappeared. She was a junior colleague in the university's archaeology department, and she acted as though he were a thief who'd disappeared into the night.

"Um," Alex said, "my mother's not here."

He started to close the door, but she put her hand out to stop it. "Let's just us talk."

In the forsaken wasteland that lay somewhere at the edge of Asgard, the meeting of the Norse gods continued. Frigga, queen of the gods, glared at Loki through teary eyes.

"When Balder died, the whole world wept, Loki. Every god in Asgard wept. Every man on earth wept. Every tree and every rock offered up their tears. Every giant and giantess cried for the death of Balder. Except you."

Her tears didn't touch the god of mischief. He simply shrugged. "I'm not the crying type."

Thor spoke, his voice rumbling like thunder. "No god should die. This is the beginning of the end."

The slim trickster god grinned. "Kill me then, and double the trouble. If that's what you want."

"I cry for my son every day!" Frigga wailed.

Thor clenched his teeth. "Loki will suffer the same."

The thunder god raised his mighty hammer. Instantly shadows rolled across the sky, quickly forming themselves into storm clouds that towered like black mountains. Lightning flashed around their peaks, and thunder rolled down to shake the ground beneath their feet.

"Thor," Loki whispered, the grin falling away from his face.

Thor ignored him. He pointed a thick, gnarled finger at Loki's family. "Vali, son of Loki!"

"No . . . ," Loki pleaded.

Thor brought his hammer down. As he did, a great shaft of lightning ripped through the clouds and struck Vali. The blow hurled Vali to the ground, where his body lay smoking and trembling. Loki's wife, Sigyn, screamed and started forward but then stopped in utter amazement.

Before her eyes, her son changed shape. Vali's strong arms grew thinner, his legs shortened, and his face stretched out. His hands turned to claws and fur sprouted from his skin. His clothes tore away, and the creature that had once been Vali sprang to its feet, snarling and snapping. Loki's son had become a wolf.

"By the giants, what have you done?" Loki demanded. His smug expression was completely gone now.

Thor glanced not at him but at Odin, who stood quietly by. Odin, father of the gods, was said to have the greatest wisdom in all the worlds. Odin gave one short, simple nod. Thor turned back to Loki. "You will suffer as Frigga suffers." The thunder god raised his hand and pointed at Narvi, Loki's other son.

Instantly the wolf sprang at Narvi, teeth bared.

Alex felt uncomfortable having Barbara Frazier in the house. He barely knew her, and what he knew he didn't like. She and his father had been colleagues, but never actually friends. Alex, in his one or two encounters with her, had always thought of her as a pencil pusher rather than a real archaeologist like his dad. Although his father would never have admitted it, Alex figured that Dr. Frazier was jealous of his success.

Unwilling to slam the door in her face, though, Alex had let her in—and then ignored her. She had followed him back to the kitchen, where he stowed the milk, and she watched him for a moment as he looked around for something to make a sandwich from, all the while hoping she would go away. But she didn't. Since the silent treatment wasn't working, he decided to take the direct approach. He turned to face her.

"What do you want here?" he demanded. "The university's insurance company is already suing us because they think Dad stole something—as if we could ever afford to pay them anyway. So what do you want?"

Barbara Frazier nodded sympathetically. "The university didn't have a choice about that."

Alex didn't buy it. There were always choices. "We could lose our house," he said angrily.

"I know. I'm sorry." She almost sounded like she meant it, but Alex didn't buy that, either.

Barbara continued. "This doesn't have to be a fight. We want the same thing."

"Yeah?" he asked. "You looking for your father too?"

She frowned. "No. I'm looking for the answer to this."

She pulled two photographs out of her purse and laid them on the kitchen counter. They were black-and-white pictures of a small statue. Even in the picture, the statue looked ancient and delicate: a tall, slender Chinese woman riding an overgrown frog. Alex recognized it—this was the jade statue his father had been examining right before he disappeared.

"If you're looking for answers," Alex said with mock sincerity, "I can tell you for a fact— that's a statue."

Dr. Frazier was not amused. "Oh, I know. I know because I've spent the last three weeks repairing it after your father smashed it to pieces. It wasn't easy, you know, picking up every fragment of the statue that had broken on the floor upstairs in your father's office. But I was able to do it. It went from priceless to worthless, of course, but at least it's back together."

"And that's why you're here?" Alex asked.

Dr. Frazier nodded. "What if I told you the reconstruction is almost eight hundred grams lighter than the original?"

"Maybe you forgot to put a new battery in it."

She didn't like this joke either. "Or maybe your father remembered to take something out of it."

Alex realized what she was suggesting and felt his face grow hot with anger. "My father's not a thief."

Dr. Frazier seemed to enjoy his reaction. She picked up the pictures and studied them for a moment, then said without glancing at him, "But you see how it looks. He smashed a priceless statue and disappeared. Now we find that he took something with him. What do you think people will say?"

"People say a lot of stuff," Alex replied.

"They'll say he did this for money, and we both know that's not true," she said. Now she did look at Alex. She looked at him so intently that he almost squirmed. "I think he found something. Something very important."

Alex swallowed. Dr. Frazier had no way of knowing how close she was to the truth. But how could he explain it to her? *"You're right, ma'am. My dad found a magical portal, and somehow got sucked into a computer-generated world of old myths and folktales. I'll go get him now. Be right back!"* Yeah, right.

Dr. Frazier misunderstood his silence. When she spoke again, there was a sharp edge to her voice. "Matt gets caught up in his work. He forgets . . . he forgets that I worked with him for six years. I should be in on this. Make sure he knows that."

Alex realized what her final comment meant. He said incredulously, "You think he's not really missing? You think I know how to reach him?"

Dr. Frazier stepped back, calming herself down. She smiled. "I think before this goes any farther, someone needs to remind him that we're supposed to be a team. I'm not getting cut out of this."

The wolf that had been Vali raised its bloody head and howled. Then it turned away from the fallen body of Narvi, its blood lust seemingly satisfied. The creature cast an eye on Freya and snarled.

Thor stepped in front of the enchanted wolf and raised his hammer. Instantly the wolf whined, its tail drooping between its legs. The creature gave one final, piteous yelp at the assembled Norse gods, then fled.

Sigyn, meanwhile, had fallen to her knees beside the lifeless body of Narvi. She threw back her dark cloak and shook him. "Narvi!" she cried, weeping helplessly, but it was clear that he was gone. With tears in her eyes, she looked up at Thor. "Why?"

The thunder god was unmoved by her cries. "Loki took a son of Odin," he declared. "He pays with a son."

Loki trembled with anger. He looked as though he wanted to throw himself at Thor, but he knew that would accomplish nothing. Thor was a god who wrestled with giants. To fight him hand to hand would be worse than useless. But Loki had other weapons.

"You know how this ends," he said ominously. "When I am free, you all die."

Thor would not listen. Grimly, he reached

down into the body of Narvi and pulled out what looked like a tangle of slimy red chains. He raised his hands to the sky: Narvi's intestines! Gripping his gruesome prize, he stalked toward Loki.

Chapter Three

"Ow!"

Cleo Bellows sat on a weight bench, her arm straining to lift a dumbbell. Several strands of her long brown hair had slipped free of her ponytail and fallen in front of her eyes and mouth. She blew them away with a grunt and forced the bar all the way down. Once the bar reached her legs, she let it go. The heavy plates slammed back with a loud clang.

"Nice work!" said Josh Beineke, her physical therapist. "Just two more reps."

"You've got to be kidding," Cleo groaned.

Josh grinned. "It wouldn't be so hard when you come to the office if you'd do them at home. Are you exercising the way we talked about?"

"Some," she grunted, trying to pull the bar down again. *Clang!*

"The mouth lies," Josh said, "the muscles don't."

Clang! "The weights lie," Cleo gasped. "That has got to be twice as heavy as it's supposed to be."

Josh laughed again. He had a nice laugh, Cleo thought. It probably served him well with most of his clients who were physically challenged—like her. Cleo had lost the use of her legs long ago in a stupid childhood accident. It was a fall, the kind of fall that probably happens to a thousand kids a week all over the country, but the minute she'd hit the ground her legs had gone numb. She hadn't been able to move them since.

Josh raised the bar and Cleo slid off the weight bench and into her wheelchair. Josh, who had a face full of smile lines, laughed at everything. He laughed on the days when she was determined to improve her strength, and he laughed on the days when she complained about her exercises.

He kneeled next to Cleo and began to bend and straighten her left leg. "Busy with school lately?"

"Not so much school," Cleo said. "Things. Other stuff. I have a life, you know."

He snorted. "Inside the computer."

Cleo's breath caught for a moment. *Inside the computer.* What did he mean by that?

"It's not good for anyone to spend too much time chatting at the keyboard," Josh continued.

By the time he'd finished his sentence, Cleo had already started to calm down. Of course Josh Beineke had no knowledge of the secret she and her brother, Alex, shared. He had no idea that the phrase "inside the computer" was more than just an expression to them. It was something real. Alex had actually gone inside, to some other place . . . to an Alterworld.

Josh frowned at her leg, unhappy about something he was feeling in Cleo's stiff muscles. He switched to the other leg and began the same bend-and-straighten routine. "You know, if you're not doing this every night, you might as well not be doing it."

It was Cleo's turn to snort. "If I could do that every night, I wouldn't be here."

Josh laughed.

Most people saw Cleo's wheelchair as a curse. Some of them even asked her how it felt to be "trapped" in it. But Cleo didn't feel trapped at all. Her wheelchair was her freedom. It made her mobile. When she wanted to be, she was all flashing chrome and spokes—doing sixty revolutions per minute down a sidewalk, popping wheelies and making spins. Of course, she'd have traded every trick she knew for a good long walk, but that sort of trade was impossible, so Cleo had settled for amateur stunt-chair work.

That afternoon, she performed some of her coolest tricks in the upstairs den of her house, rocking back and spinning around as Alex told her the story of Dr. Frazier's visit.

". . . and on top of blaming Dad for breaking that statue, now they're going to start saying he took whatever was hidden inside. That he ran off with some gold nugget or something."

Cleo let her wheelchair fall forward with a clunk. "We know that's not what happened." She looked at her brother. "What'd Mom say when you told her?"

Alex shrugged. "She kind of got really quiet, and then she went for a drive."

Cleo knew what it meant when Mom went for a drive. "She lost it."

"Yup."

"Do you think she's going to be okay?"

Alex said, "I don't even know if *I'm* going to be okay. I mean, I'd pretty much freak out if Dad really did run off with some kind of ancient treasure. But this . . ." His voice trailed off as he looked at the high-tech computer setup their father had designed. There were the standard keyboard and monitor, but that wasn't what made the computer interesting. Set against a wall was a special holographic plasma screen that produced three-dimensional images of anything scanned into the computer. There was also a microphone on the desktop that allowed the user to enter the voice commands the computer followed.

Cleo rolled her chair a bit closer. "Are we . . . are we going to do this?"

Alex moved in but was careful not to touch the plasma screen. The last time he'd done that, he'd found himself transported to ancient Greece—only it wasn't the historical Greece, it was the Greece of ancient mythology. Alex had become Theseus, a legendary Greek hero, and had had to fight a ferocious creature called the Minotaur. Sometimes he still heard its screams when he slept.

"I've got to tell you, I'm not so crazy about trying this again to see what monster's waiting for me this time."

Cleo said, "But if that's where Dad is . . ."

Alex felt his mouth go dry. "If Dad's in there, let's hope he didn't meet up with the Minotaur."

Cleo spun her chair to face him. "Look, I'm scared too, but we can't just do nothing, and there aren't any other choices. All we know is that there's a door or something here that takes us to another world, and our father vanished through it."

"And some guy named Gorgos might know what happened to him."

Gorgos. Neither of them had mentioned that name since Alex's first adventure in the Alterworld. They knew nothing about this mysterious figure. He had been the only person in the Greek myth who seemed to know that Alex wasn't really Theseus. In fact, he seemed to know all about Alex's father. Gorgos had enjoyed Alex's fear. Just thinking of the creature made his skin crawl.

Cleo broke the brief silence. "You know, I looked him up. There's nothing on Gorgos in any of the sources I found online." That was odd, because every other artifact in the 3D museum was related to a well-known ancient myth. She added, "If he is a mythological creature, he's so old his stories have been forgotten." She returned to the same conclusion she'd reached a moment ago. "It looks like the only way we're going to find out any more is by trying it again ourselves."

"That's easy for you to say," Alex said. He regretted it instantly. It wasn't Cleo's fault she was in a wheelchair, and he knew she would volunteer to go into the Alterworld if she were able.

He was grateful when his sister decided to

ignore the comment. She wheeled herself over to a nearby shelf cluttered with an odd assortment of books, computer disks, and age-old pieces of carved stone. "You know," she mused aloud, "not everything Dad scanned in was on loan from big museums." She picked up a stone bowl. It was shallow and rough. On one side, they could just make out a green stain, the remains of a faded design. "Some of this stuff Dad collected himself. I wonder . . ."

Cleo whirled around and glided over to the computer. She spoke into the microphone. "Stone bowls, room two."

The computer responded with a short beep. The plasma screen lit up, and the Bellows siblings watched as the screen displayed fifteen stone bowls.

Cleo used a computer mouse to sort through the various stone bowls onscreen until she found one that matched the fragment in her hand. Actually, the computer had used her fragment to create an artist's rendering of the whole bowl.

"There's the scan of what this bowl would have looked like."

The scan was actually cleaner than the real artifact. In the computer, they could see the original design etched into the fragment—a snake winding its way around the rim of the container.

Alex tried to follow his sister's reasoning. "So you think this is going to lead me to Dad?"

Cleo gave him a look that said, *Do you have any better ideas?* Then she spoke. "I think it's got a shot. At least it's something he cared about."

Alex was still skeptical. "What if I can't get back?"

"I think I've got that part figured out," his sister said, brightening a bit. "Last time, you went into the Greek myth when you touched the scan of that gold pendant of Dionysus, the Greek god. And when you touched the same thing on the other side, you came back."

"Yeah, I was there. I got that," Alex said.

"So get this." Cleo pulled a plastic bag from her lap and dropped the fragment of the stone bowl into it. "Take this with you. Anything over there gets too hairy, you just reach in, touch this, and zip, you're home. Do not pass Go, do not collect two hundred dollars."

Alex hesitated. But really, there was nothing else to be done. Their father was gone, and this was their only lead. He nodded and took the plastic bag back from his sister.

Turning, Alex stood before the plasma screen. He reached out to the three-dimensional image of the snake bowl and touched it. There was a flash of light and Alex Bellows was gone . . .

. . . and the bowl fragment inside the plastic bag dropped to the ground.

Cleo watched the bag fall to the floor and her eyes opened wide in fear. The fragment hadn't gone through. Her plan had failed. Whatever mystical power opened the gateway to the Alterworld, it would not send any objects through, only people. Which meant Alex was trapped. Again.

Chapter Four

It wasn't any easier the second time around.

The feeling of being wrenched out of the real world was like the stomach-dropping sensation of a roller coaster ride—except that it wasn't your stomach you left behind, it was your brain.

Alex didn't feel anything physical. There was no tingling, no heat, no sense of his atoms being ripped apart and reassembled somewhere. Physically, he felt fine.

But inside his skull his brain was bending

around itself, trying to make sense of something that was absolutely impossible.

A split second ago, Alex had been standing in his father's home office. But in this split second, he suddenly found himself . . . somewhere else. He was standing on some kind of rocky plateau at the edge of a mountain. The land around him was gray, and overhead the sun cast a pale yellow light. A chill wind whispered sadly over the ground.

Nearby, Alex saw a small pool of water and walked toward it. His heart had already stopped racing, and his brain was settling down to the fact that, impossible as it was, he was definitely somewhere else now, and he would just have to deal with it. In fact, after a few steps Alex had almost completely calmed down.

Maybe this does get easier, he thought.

But as he reached the pool, Alex slowed down, resisting the urge to look at his reflection in the water. He wasn't sure what he would see, but he did know one thing: it wouldn't be him. The last time Alex had crossed over into the Alterworld, he had become Theseus. On that trip, everyone Alex met in the Alterworld had seen him as Theseus. He was sure it would be the same here. He just didn't know what sort of person he'd be.

Alex knelt down beside the pool and slowly leaned forward until he could see his reflection in the still water. The person he saw looking back at him was nothing like Alex Bellows. It was a young man with dark hair and a tortured face. Instead of the T-shirt and jeans that were Alex's daily uniform, his reflection wore a thick wool shirt trimmed with fur.

The face and the shirt were covered with blood.

"Ah!" Alex looked down at his arms and saw that they too were covered with blood. He plunged them into the water and began to scrub. "Ah! I'm all covered in—" He couldn't bring himself to say it. "What did I do?"

"You didn't do anything."

Alex nearly jumped out of his skin. It was Cleo's voice, the sound reaching him out of nowhere. In his sudden terror at the sight of so much blood covering him, Alex had nearly forgotten one of the most important aspects of his adventure in the Alterworld. Cleo could see him. By watching the plasma-screen images back in their father's office, his sister could see his progress through the myths in which he appeared. And, more importantly, he could hear her voice when she spoke into the computer's voice command microphone.

Alex looked up, although, of course, he could not see Cleo at all. He said in near panic, "L-look at me. I'm covered in blood!"

"That's not you," Cleo reminded him, trying to sound calm and reassuring. "That's whoever you're filling in for."

"Well." Alex snorted, slowly regaining his composure. "It's still disgusting. And it's still on me."

He knelt down beside the pool again and tried to wash the blood away. The water in the pool was as cold as ice. "This is freezing. Which makes me think I'm not in Hawaii. So where am I, Iceland?"

"It could be Norway," Cleo's voice came back. "According to Dad's database, that stone bowl is a Viking artifact."

Alex cupped his hands and brought a splash of the frigid water up to his face. He gasped as the coldness hit his skin and he felt icy beads of water run down his neck. When he looked at his reflection again, the blood was gone from around his mouth. He said, "Yeah, speaking of that bowl, Cleo . . ."

"I know, I know," Cleo shot back. "I'm sorry. It's here."

"That's a giant help, thanks," he said dryly.

"I should have known nothing would go through. Since your clothes change and everything about you changes, it's like only you get to go, not the things you take with you."

Alex nodded. "Well, I always did like to pack light."

He chuckled, and as if in answer to his laugh, a long, deep-throated wail of pure agony rose up from the ground. A second later, as the inhuman scream continued to echo among the rocks, the earth began to tremble. The quake threw Alex off his feet, and he clutched at a few tufts of grass. The ground bucked once, twice, three times, nearly bouncing Alex back up to his feet. An instant later the screaming stopped, and the ground subsided at almost the exact same moment.

"Um, okay, it's either Norway or San Francisco," Alex said, still lying on his stomach clutching the grass. Since the earthquake had died down, he pulled himself up and dusted off his strange, thick, woolen clothes. Other than the barren gray rocks and the steep mountainside, the only feature that stood out was the cave.

"I think the screaming came from over there." He stopped and considered. "Now there's a sentence you really don't want to hear."

"It's better than hearing the screams," Cleo pointed out.

"I guess I'd better go check it out."

Alex trudged over to the cave. As he walked, he was reminded of how strange the concept of being someone else was. Alex felt completely like himself—he thought and moved exactly as he always did. But anyone who met him in this Alterworld would see him as the haunted-looking young man he'd stared at in the pool.

Alex reached the cave entrance. The faint sunlight stopped there; just a few feet past the portal, all was lost in darkness. He took one step forward, then hesitated, his foot just inside the entryway.

"Tell me this isn't crazy," he groaned.

"What do you mean?" Cleo replied, her voice like a whisper in his ear.

"Last time, I had no idea what I was getting myself into. I mean, I just touched the screen and suddenly I was Theseus."

"Yeah, and?"

"And I'd have to be crazy to touch the screen again and wind up who knows where. We don't even know who I am or what I'm supposed to be doing."

He couldn't see Cleo, but he heard the frustration in her voice. "You're looking for Dad. He's got to be in there somewhere."

Alex hoped so. But neither of them knew. Still, there was absolutely nothing else to do. "Hello?" he called out, so softly that he could barely hear himself. He licked his lips and realized that his mouth had gone dry. Someone in that cave had screamed—and, more importantly, something had *made* someone scream like that. Alex gathered himself together and said, louder this time, "Hello!"

"Son?"

The voice came out of the darkness, faint and distorted by echoes. Hearing that word made Alex's heart skip a beat. "It can't be. Dad?"

From out of the real world, Cleo's voice echoed his own. "Dad!"

Forgetting the screams and the danger, Alex charged into the darkness.

Chapter Five

Entering the cave, Alex realized that it wasn't nearly as dark as he'd thought it would be. His eyes adjusted almost immediately, and he found himself running down a tunnel that opened up into a huge cavern. The underground chamber was bathed in a soft light, fainter than the weak sun outside but bright enough to illuminate the room.

What Alex saw in that dim light stopped him in his tracks.

In the middle of the cavern, stretched over

the top of three clustered rocks, a man lay bound. His dark red shackles seemed to glow with a life of their own. A woman stood beside the man, holding a stone bowl over his head. At first, Alex thought she was offering him something to drink, but she did not move the bowl from its place in midair. A moment later, a perfect teardrop of some pale liquid fell from the ceiling and splashed into the bowl.

Alex looked until his eyes lit upon a sight as terrifying as the Minotaur. A serpent hung coiled around a stalactite hanging from the ceiling, its writhing head hovering in the air, mouth open in a prolonged and terrible hiss. Two long fangs jutted from its mouth, and Alex could see a drop of venom forming at the end of one. He said nothing as the venom grew into a heavy drop, then fell through the air to land in the bowl with a faint *plop*.

Neither the chained man nor the woman seemed to notice Alex at first, so he watched a moment longer. Another venom drop formed, and the woman caught this one as well, but the sound of the splash told Alex that the bowl was full. Even as he thought this, the woman turned away and carried the bowl to a shadowy corner of the cavern, where she emptied the vessel into a hole in the ground. She hurried back, but she was too late. Another drop of venom had already fallen. The poison struck the chained man on the cheek, and a wisp of smoke rose up from the spot as though he'd been burned by acid.

The chained man let out a heart-wrenching cry of pain.

"Who—what is this?" Alex asked.

In the middle of a scream, the prisoner turned his head to the side and stared directly at Alex. Beside him, the woman smiled beneath her dark cloak. "It's Vali! He's all right!"

Alex didn't know who Vali was. He didn't care. He was suddenly bombarded with emotions—disappointment that he had not found his father, relief that his father wasn't the one being tortured, and horror at the sight of such cruelty. He pointed at the prisoner and said, "What—what's happened?"

The chained man lifted his head. A spot on his forehead still smoked from the venom, but to Alex's horror and surprise, there wasn't a mark on him. "It's not your fault, son," the man said weakly. "Even gods like us play the parts that Fate writes for us. Nothing else could have happened. Nothing else ever will."

The man let his head fall back onto the stone as more drops of venom fell. The woman caught them until her bowl filled again. As she turned away, more poison splashed onto the man's face. He let out another howl of agony, and the earth shook to its core.

Alex clapped his hands over his ears and cringed.

Lily Bellows had walked down the hallway of the university's archaeology department hundreds of times, but today it felt alien. Today she was visiting her husband's offices for the first time since he'd disappeared. She had avoided the place. Not coming here, she'd been able to pretend, somehow, that he was still around—not at home but at the office, working late. There had been times in the past, when he was on an intense project, that he'd arrive home after she went to bed and be up in the morning before she opened her eyes.

Now, as she hurried down the hallways of the old brick building, she realized that she'd been pretending that all along. But coming here made her face the reality that her husband had vanished.

She stopped in front of a door, its upper half made of frosted glass. The words DR. MATTHEW BELLOWS were stenciled into the glass.

Next to it was a smaller door, windowless. A sheet of paper was taped to the door. It read: DR. BARBARA I. FRAZIER.

Lily Bellows knocked on that door, but there was no answer. "Barbara!" she called. Still no answer.

At the same moment, the door of her husband's office opened and Barbara Frazier appeared. Lily took a step back, startled. "Barbara? What are you doing?"

Barbara Frazier glanced back into Dr. Bellows's office with a definite look of guilt. She erased it with a cough and said, "Oh, um, just boxing up some stuff."

"In Matt's office?"

Barbara Frazier stiffened. "I need more space. Come on, Lily, someone has to fill in for Matt. The department doesn't run itself."

Lily glared at Barbara but didn't know what to say. She had never gotten along with this woman. Her husband had liked Barbara well enough. He always said that he'd spent eleven months unwrapping a single Egyptian mummy to find its heart. Barbara Frazier couldn't be that much harder.

Finally, Barbara broke the silence. "You were looking for me?"

Lily said coldly, "Alex told me you were at the house today."

Barbara's face lost some of its color. "Oh."

"You've got a hell of a nerve coming to my house and bothering my kids," Lily said angrily. "You want to discuss Matt, you talk to me."

"You are a hundred percent right. It won't happen again."

Lily bit her lip. She had been expecting denials, or excuses, or something. She hadn't expected an apology. Anger was still roiling inside her, but now she had nowhere to aim it.

Barbara said tentatively, "Did Alex tell you what we talked about?"

"Yes," Lily replied.

"What do *you* think happened?"

Lily resented this line of questioning. This woman had no right to pry into an affair that was so personal and so painful to the Bellows family.

But the fact was that Lily didn't know what had happened. Her entire world had been altered by her husband's sudden disappearance, and she had no idea what to make of it. She was being sued by her husband's university, her catering business was swallowing more and more time, and the police were stopping by her house every few days with more questions than answers.

Lily's shoulders slumped and she sighed wearily. She said, "You know Matt's work better than anyone. You studied this statue. Do you think . . . ?"

"Do I think there was something inside?" Barbara said, finishing the question. "Yes, I do."

Lily shook her head in disbelief. "Something so important that it would make Matt forget his family?"

Barbara nodded. "Something that would make any archaeologist in the world forget his family, his research, his duty to his colleagues."

The cold certainty in Barbara's voice made Lily shiver. For the first time, she considered the possibility that her husband had run away for good.

Chapter Six

"Aaaarrrgh!"

Another drop of venom splashed in the chained man's face, and another scream shook the foundations of the world. The prisoner's screams were driving Alex insane. He glanced up at the serpent, its dark body gleaming in the strange light that filled the cavern. Desperately, he looked around for some weapon.

The woman, returning with her empty bowl, said sadly, "Don't worry, Loki. I'm here. Vali's here. We won't leave you."

Alex found a large round rock and hefted it. "Let me just get rid of that thing." He looked up again, measuring the distance to the dangling snake.

"You can't!" the woman said.

"I've got pretty good aim," Alex said.

The woman took one hand off the bowl to touch Alex's shoulder. "No. The gods put it there. It's magical. You can't destroy it with a rock."

A voice spoke in Alex's ear. It was Cleo. "I found some stuff on Viking mythology."

"It's about time," Alex whispered into the air. "Because I'm about to go crazy here."

There was a pause, and Alex guessed that his sister was reading through some text she'd found. Because Cleo was back in the real world watching all this on the plasma screen, she could also use the Internet to research whatever Alex encountered. A moment later, she said, "Okay, the woman is named Sigyn. Her husband is that guy on the rocks—his name is Loki. He's the Norse god of, I don't know, con artists."

To anyone else, it might have sounded strange to be told that the person you'd just met was a Norse god. Since Alex had already been ripped out of the real world and into this alternate reality twice, and he'd already faced a monster that was half-man and half-bull, the idea of an ancient mythological god wasn't hard to swallow.

"Okay, so how'd he wind up here?"

"Checking," Cleo replied. "Um . . . oh, that's disgusting."

"What?"

"Oh, man. According to this text I found, the gods turned Loki's son, Vali—that's you—into a wolf, and Vali killed his brother, Narvi."

"Turned into a wolf? But I'm not a wolf now."

"It's a myth, Alex," Cleo reminded him. "I guess you turned back." She went on. "Anyway, then the gods used Narvi's entrails for the chains."

"Entrails?"

"His, um, guts."

"Gross," Alex said. "The gods did this to him? Why?"

He spoke the words loudly enough for the woman, Sigyn, to hear. She thought he was talking to her. "They had to blame someone," she said. "They chose your father."

Alex felt his face flush with anger. That was exactly what was happening to his real father. An ancient artifact was missing. The police and the university had to blame someone, and they'd chosen his dad.

"That's not right," he said.

Sigyn shrugged. "It happens all the time. You know how they are."

Alex, still thinking more of home than of this world, said, "Yeah. They'd rather think a guy they liked and trusted is a criminal than admit they don't know *what* happened."

He didn't know anything about this Loki, but he did know he was tired of people looking for scapegoats. He grabbed hold of the chains and pulled, but they wouldn't budge. "I'm getting you out of here," he said.

"Let it be, Vali," Loki said.

Alex picked up the rock again and brought it down hard on the chains. Sparks flew, but the chains were undamaged. "They won't break!" he growled. He banged at the chains again in frustration. As he did, his arm brushed against Sigyn, knocking her hands away as she tried to catch the next drop of venom. The poison spilled on Alex's arm instead. He felt a brief moment of searing pain, as if someone had splashed fire onto his skin. Alex nearly screamed as he leaped back from the rocks, clutching at his arm. The pain subsided quickly, but the memory of it made his skin tingle.

Sigyn frowned sadly at him. "Now you see why I stand here. To catch as much as I can. It's our fate."

Alex looked at his arm where the venom had splashed. The burn was already fading. That must be one of the advantages of being a god—nothing could hurt him for long. But in Loki's case, that gift was more like a curse. That meant he could be tortured like this forever.

"No one deserves to be treated this way," Alex said. "What could he possibly have done?"

"It doesn't matter what he *did*," Sigyn said as though talking to a naive young boy. "It's what the others *think* he did. The god Balder was killed. Another god did the deed, but Loki takes the blame. Now we are all condemned."

Sigyn's words struck close to home. She might have been describing Alex's father, not Loki. "There's got to be a way out of this," Alex said.

Sigyn shook her head. "He'll lie here forever. I'll hold this bowl forever."

Alex gritted his teeth in determination. Sigyn had given up, but for him giving up was never an option. His father had taught him that. There was a solution to every problem, an answer to every mystery. It was only a question of whether you were willing to work hard enough to find it.

"There has to be another way," he said. He looked at the chains. "Somebody made these chains. Somebody can unmake them."

Alex expected Cleo to pipe up with more details about this myth, but instead Sigyn offered a suggestion. "It would take Thor's hammer."

"No!" Loki sputtered. He raised his head from the rocks again, a wild and fearful look in his eyes. "No! I already lost one son today. I won't lose another."

"The hammer is called Mjollner. It can break anything," Sigyn added.

"Okay," Alex said determinedly. "Okay, so where do I find it?"

"Across the Rainbow Bridge," Sigyn said. "In Asgard, the home of the gods."

Alex glanced at Loki. The chained god looked as if he wanted to protest, but he was too weak from pain. His head fell back against the rocks and rolled to one side as he lost consciousness. Alex's heart nearly broke. He didn't know who this Loki really was, but he was someone's father and he needed help.

Alex might not be able to find his real father yet, but he could help this one. "Maybe I'll be back," he said. Then he turned and walked away.

In the cave, unseen by Alex or by Loki, who was still unconscious, the concerned expression on Sigyn's face suddenly changed to a cynical leer. Her voice became an evil, distorted growl. If Alex had heard that voice, he might have guessed who it was.

"Yes," Gorgos said slyly. "Go get the hammer. I can't wait to see what happens."

Chapter Seven

Alex walked out of the dim cave and into the pale sunlight. It was cold. He shivered and pulled his clothes tight around him, glad his shirt was made of thick wool.

"Cleo, you there?"

For a moment there was no answer. "Cleo?"

"Hey, Alex, I'm back."

"Where'd you go?" he asked. He was getting used to talking to thin air and having her respond. It wasn't much different from talking on a speaker phone.

"In a minute. What are you doing now?"

"I guess I'm going to find Thor's hammer."

There was a pause. "Uh, Alex, how does that help us find Dad?"

It doesn't, Alex admitted to himself. Aloud, he said, "Well, I'm not going to find him by standing here. And I'm not going to leave Loki there just because he's not who I was looking for. Maybe Thor will know about Dad."

He stood stubbornly waiting for her to respond. Cleo was good at giving lectures when she set her mind to it, and Alex expected one now. But she just said, "I was on the phone with Mom. You'll never guess where she went."

Alex chuckled. "If it's not Norway, I'm not impressed."

"She had a chat with Barbara Frazier."

Alex felt himself tense up, like the feeling he got when a dog barked at him from the other side of a fence. He knew there was no real danger, but it made him worry anyway. "You don't think Mom told her anything?"

"She doesn't know anything to tell, Alex," his sister reminded him.

"And it's a good thing. Mom's pretty much the worst liar in the world."

"But I hate not being able to tell her about all this."

Alex started walking, although he didn't know where he was going. Anywhere was better than the mouth of that cave. He walked down a barren path that seemed to lead out of the mountains. "You know she'd never let us do this, even if she did believe us."

"Do you know where you're going?" Cleo suddenly asked.

"Loki's wife said to cross the Rainbow Bridge to Asgard. Although I'm not sure if I'm supposed to be looking for a heart or some courage," he joked.

"What you need is brains," Cleo cracked back, catching his *Wizard of Oz* joke. "In fact, while you've been playing with snakes, I've done some checking. Asgard is one of the nine worlds of Norse mythology. The kingdom of the gods. Midgard is where men live. Helheim is the realm of the dead. Utgard is where the giants are."

"I thought the Giants were in New York," Alex said.

"You want the info or not?" his sister said, groaning at his sense of humor.

"Okay, I get the picture. What about the Rainbow Bridge?"

There was a pause as Cleo checked her research. "Not a lot of detail on that."

"Great," Alex said sarcastically. "Now what am I supposed to—"

He stopped in midsentence. He had been walking, and as he rounded a curve in the path, he suddenly found himself staring at a brilliant wall of shimmering colors. The colors were bright, like the colored lights of a theater stage, but there were no lamps anywhere and these lights didn't hurt his eyes the way electrical lights did. The lights were soft and warm, and the colors were amazingly clear. Most astonishing of all, Alex could not find any source. The colors seemed to rise out of the ground and streak into the sky. Or maybe it was the other way around, with the colors falling in streams from the air and blending into the earth.

It was another beautiful, impossible vision of the Alterworld, and Alex had to remind himself yet again that he was not in the historical past. He was inside a myth.

"Okay," he whispered. "You think there's a pot of gold around here somewhere?"

Without waiting for a reply from Cleo, he moved forward. But before he could reach the lights, a massive figure stepped through the rainbow colors as though passing through a thin curtain. He was clad in white fur and leather, and he scowled at Alex from behind his thick gray beard.

"Halt!"

Alex jumped back in surprise. "Okay. Definitely not in Kansas anymore."

Alarmed, he took another step back from the imposing figure. Alex was glad to hear Cleo whisper in his ear: "His name is Heimdall, the White God. He guards the entrance to Asgard. Only gods are allowed in."

"Who goes there?" Heimdall growled.

"Uh, it's—it's . . . ," Alex stammered, trying to remember his name in this myth. "Vali. It's Vali."

Heimdall squinted. His eyes seemed to see right through Alex. "Vali, son of Loki?"

"That's me," Alex said, straightening up and trying to appear godlike.

"What brings you to Asgard?"

Alex kept his chin up, but he shifted his feet nervously. "I'm looking for Thor."

Heimdall snorted. "He's in a foul mood to-day, that one. What do you want him for?"

"I need his help. To free my father."

Heimdall responded with a roar of laughter. The sound was picked up by the hills around them, so that it seemed to Alex as if the very rocks were laughing at him. After a full minute Heimdall settled down to a low chuckle, wiped a tear from his eye, and said, "You're Loki's son, all right. He could always get a laugh out of me."

Alex remembered the sight of Loki being tormented and set his jaw in determination. "I'm not laughing."

Heimdall's sharp eyes widened. "You're serious?" He shook his head so hard that the tips of his mustache quivered. "Thor put him in that cave. He's not going to let him out anytime soon."

Alex frowned. "Oh. Um, any suggestions?"

"Did you bring any grog?"

Grog. Alex didn't know what grog was, and he certainly didn't have any. He couldn't even come through with a stone bowl!

Heimdall saw his look of confusion and said, "Loki could talk gold out of a dwarf. Maybe you've got your father's gift. Go ahead."

The strong guardian of Asgard stepped aside and motioned for Alex to move forward. The young man walked tentatively toward the shimmering curtain of colors. Then, with Heimdall nodding encouragement, he stepped through.

It felt like passing through a warm mist. Alex's skin tingled, and he blinked something bright and surprising, but not unpleasant, out of his eyes. By the time he had regained his vision, he was standing on the far side of the Rainbow Bridge.

Heimdall was gone, and so were the rocky mountains and the pale sunlight. Here it was deep winter, with snow on the ground and nothing but dark clouds overhead. Before him rose a massive granite mountain, jagged as a thunderbolt, piercing the sky. At the very top of the mountain, Alex could see the Great Hall, its high walls and strong roof framed against a wintry gray sky. Majestic as it was sitting atop the mountain, the hall also gave off a feeling of warmth and homeliness. From what little Alex knew of the Vikings, he recalled that in Norse mythology the gods were very human, beings of passion and fun as well as divine power.

"That was wild," Alex said to his unseen

sister. "Check out the geography in this place. *Whoosh!* Next stop, land of the gods!"

"Not a bad system, especially if you're late for school."

Alex nodded, knowing that Cleo could see him. "Question, though. What makes these people gods? I mean, they act like human beings. And take a look at how they're treating Loki—it's not exactly how you want a higher power to act, is it?"

"Well, maybe it's not how *we* want a higher power to act," Cleo pointed out. "But this is how the ancient Norse people saw things. They saw their gods as being bigger, stronger versions of themselves. The Norse gods were immortal, and they represented things like the weather, love, and wisdom. But they were very, very human, which means they got mad, had fights, started wars. They lied, cheated, and made mistakes."

Alex snorted. "Ancient Norway sounds a lot like where we live."

Alex started walking. After a short pause, Cleo said, "Alex, I'm not sure this is such a good idea. Maybe Thor isn't your best bet for help."

"From what I got back there, Thor's the only one who *can* help."

"How do you know?" Cleo said. "The father of the gods is Odin. He's supposed to be really wise. If you're going to ask anyone about Dad, he's your best bet. I can probably figure out where he is—"

"Okay, Cleo," Alex said. "But after I do this." He paused, glancing skyward as though looking into her eyes. "I can't explain it. Maybe it's not the same watching through the computer, but I'm here. And I can't stand that someone here is being wrongly accused."

"But Alex, it's not like you owe Loki anything." She hesitated. "He's not Dad."

Alex grunted. "He's somebody's dad. And he needs help."

Chapter Eight

The granite mountain reached up into the sky for what seemed like miles. A single narrow path wound its way up the steep slopes, zigzagging back and forth, cutting a jagged scar along the face of the peak. Halfway up the side of the mountain, Alex passed the aeries of eagles. Some nests were empty; others held fierce-looking birds of prey tucked in against their feathers, keeping out the wintry cold. He climbed higher still, through a bank of snow-laden clouds. At the top, the clouds looked like a thick blanket of snow spread out before him. The sight took his breath away.

And still he climbed, impossibly high, to where the air would have been thin if he'd been in the real world. But here he could breathe normally as he pulled himself up to the summit and stood before the hall of the Norse god of thunder.

The door of the hall was twice Alex's height and made of wood as thick as his leg. It was open—probably because the god of thunder had no need to fear anyone. Alex leaned over the threshold, his eyes scanning bare stone walls and a stone roof. Shields taller than Alex and polished to a glow lined the walls. The center of the hall was empty, except for a large fire pit that crackled with flame. Cautiously, he stepped inside and moved toward the fire. As he did, he passed one of the shields and glanced at it. The polished surface acted as a mirror, showing him his reflection. Once again he saw not himself but Vali, his face set in Alex's frown. The forehead of Vali/Alex was wrinkled with worry.

"Yeah, well, you've got things to worry about," Alex told his reflection. "Sure, just go get Thor's hammer. No problem. Like the god of thunder has nothing better to do."

Alex took another step. "Like the god of thunder's not going to just drive his hammer through my skull when I tell him why I came."

As Alex moved another furtive step into the hall, a man appeared at the other end of the great room, followed by three or four women with braided blond hair. The man was massive, so tall and broad that he made the room seem suddenly small. In one hand he clutched a huge drinking horn. He brought it up and threw back his head, gulping the contents in a single effort. He wiped his mouth on his sleeve and thrust the horn toward one of the women. "Refill! Now!"

Alex heard Cleo whisper in his ear. "That's—"

"Thor. Yeah, I got it," Alex replied.

Taking a deep breath, Alex stepped forward where he could be seen more clearly in the firelight. "Hello?" he said.

Thor had just taken another swig from his drinking horn, and now he stopped in midgulp. He stared at Alex over the rim of the horn, then lowered it with a sound that was somewhere between a sigh and a growl. "Vali," Thor said in that same half-pleasant, half-angry voice. It occurred to Alex that the sound was exactly the sound of distant, rolling thunder.

"Hi," he said, not knowing how to address a god.

Thor growled. "You came here? To my home?" He glanced at his Valkyries. "Out! Leave us alone!" He waved an arm as thick as a tree trunk and the women scattered. Thor then turned back to Alex and started forward.

It was like watching a mountain move. Thor strode toward him, covering the entire length of the hall in a few steps, standing so close that his enormous chest filled Alex's field of vision. In an instant, Thor pounced and gathered Alex up into a smothering bear hug, lifting the young man off his feet as though he weighed no more than a pillow.

"You crazy kid!" Thor said, his voice booming happily throughout his hall.

"Urk," Alex said. Thor's embrace was nearly crushing the life out of him. Finally, the thunder god let go, and Alex's feet touched the ground again.

"Come! Drink with me, Vali! Nectar of the gods!"

Thor thrust a second drinking horn under Alex's nose, and he was suddenly assaulted by the smell of something that had fermented into a powerful drink. *Grog*. It made his eyes water.

Cleo's voice buzzed in his ear. "Hey, guess what? Turns out Thor and Loki were friends."

"Oh, yeah? Thanks for the news flash," Alex whispered.

"A toast to lost gods!" Thor bellowed. He lifted his horn and drained it again, ignoring the fact that Alex hadn't taken a drink.

Cleo chimed in. "Thor's the son of Odin, king of the gods. He's the strongest god; he protects Asgard and the Aesir—that's the good guys. Loki's not exactly one of them. Odin kind of adopted him. They all used to travel together. Have adventures. Guy stuff. Maybe you should play the nostalgia card here."

Alex nodded. His sister really was talented, and he didn't know what he would do without her. Having her at the computer, and being able to hear her voice, was like having a second brain he could access at any moment.

He suggested, "Uh, to Loki?"

Thor's eyes moistened for a moment and he

nodded vigorously. "To Loki. A great friend."
He drank again.

Alex hadn't missed the sad look in the thunder god's face. "You miss him, huh?"

Thor nodded again and held up his right arm, his clenched fist the size of a bowling ball. "He was my right arm. I never would have made it out of that nest of giants in Utgard without his fast talk. Or the time my hammer got stolen . . ."

The thunder god heaved an enormous sigh, his eyes drifting off toward the walls. At first Alex thought he was just daydreaming, but after a moment of silence he realized that Thor was actually looking at something. He followed the huge figure's gaze and found himself staring at one of the massive shields on the wall. The bright reflection in the shield fogged over for a moment, and suddenly it was replaced by a different scene. Inside the shield it was no longer winter—the sky was blue and the sun shone warmly. Bright-colored banners hung from the walls. A table was piled high with platters of meat and bowls of fruit. The fire in the fire pit still burned, giving off more light than warmth. Alex wasn't sure how, but he knew that it was warm inside the image.

Alex might have thought what he saw on the shield was like television, but it was more. There was a sense of reality about it, as though it could be touched. And although he was looking into the shield, he had the powerful sensation that he could reach out and touch the objects in it. He was reminded of watching real actors in a play rather than images on television.

Thor appeared in the image—a younger Thor dressed in bright, festive colors. But his face was grim. "My hammer is gone!" the image cried out.

The real Thor—the one standing next to Alex—stretched out his hand, then gripped it tight as though pulling the image toward him. For an instant, the blink of an eye, Alex felt his world turn inside out. And then he found himself standing *inside* the image.

Chapter Nine

The transformation was strange. In some ways, it was more disconcerting than the Rainbow Bridge, because there it had been clear to Alex that he had gone to a different *place*. But here, the place was the same. Alex knew he was still standing in Thor's Great Hall. But he was equally certain that he was now in a different *time*. It was summer instead of winter. The place was vibrant with summer colors, and the Thor who moved about the room seemed younger— not in years, but in his experience. Alex was sure that somehow he'd gone back in time, as if slipping backward into one of Thor's memories.

Oh, here we go again, he thought. *Just when I'm getting used to traveling to the Alterworld, now I'm going on another trip?*

Alex wasn't sure how to keep it straight. *It's easy,* he told himself. *I'm inside a story that's inside a story.* That made him feel a little better.

What made the journey most confusing was that the real Thor—Alex's Thor—was still there, standing right beside him, watching the scene just as Alex watched it. There were two Thors to watch. One of them was the real Thor—the one Alex had met first. The other was Thor from the past. That was the one they were watching.

Alex looked at the real Thor, whom he started to think of as tour-guide Thor. The god shook his head. "To this day," he said, "I don't know how it happened. I'm the only one who can lift that hammer without these gloves."

Thor stuck a thumb in his belt, and for the first time Alex noticed a pair of thick leather gloves hanging there.

Alex turned his attention back to the vision. In it, the brightly dressed Thor called out, "Father! Loki!" His voice thundered through the hall, demanding Alex's attention. Even as he looked up, other gods came running into the hall, all dressed in summer clothes, all looking majestic and magnificent. One of the gods who entered, running right past Alex, was Loki.

"But th-that's—" Alex stammered. "I mean, he's—"

Tour-guide Thor patted Alex on the arm. "They don't see you, Vali. You weren't there that day."

"But how?" Alex said, unable to form a coherent sentence. "We're . . . I mean . . ." He gathered his thoughts, but he decided to speak to Cleo instead of Thor. "I'm seriously confused. I could use some help here."

Thor thought Alex was talking to him and said matter-of-factly, "This has already happened."

Finally, Alex heard Cleo's voice in his ear. "It's wyrd."

"I'll say it's weird!" Alex cried.

Thor nodded. "Exactly."

Cleo laughed. "Thor thinks you understand. I don't mean *weird,* I mean *wyrd* with a *y.* It's kind of like fate. Wyrd is a concept from Norse mythology to describe how things are inevitable. The Vikings believed that whatever happens already is, whether it happened in the past or will happen in the future."

Alex recalled something Loki had said to him. "We play the parts the gods write for us."

"Exactly right," Cleo said.

Beside him, Thor nodded. "Then and now. Watch."

I get it, Alex told himself. *It's a flashback. I've entered a myth. And inside the myth, I've gone into someone's memory. Weird.* He settled back to watch, feeling like an eavesdropper since he was actually there, in the room. But no one seemed to notice, so he soon forgot. The Norse gods were debating who could have stolen Thor's hammer. Suddenly, Loki wiggled himself into the middle of the debate.

"Freya," he said to a goddess with a beautiful face, who was draped in a cloak made of birds' feathers. "Freya, lend me your falcon cloak. I'll fly over the nine worlds and find the hammer."

Freya said eagerly, "To get back Thor's hammer? I'd lend you anything I have!"

She unclasped the cloak from her neck and removed it gracefully. With a dramatic spin of the feathered cape, Loki wrapped it around himself and jumped like an acrobat onto the table. "In nine beats of my wings, I'll return!" he promised.

Then he leaped up—and in that instant the mischievous god vanished and a falcon flapped its wings in the air, streaking out of a nearby window.

Alex's jaw dropped. Even for a myth this was pretty amazing stuff. He wanted to talk to Cleo, not Thor. Before he could utter a single word, the falcon swooped back into the room. It flapped its wings furiously, hovering over the table. Then, in the midst of that flapping, the bird of prey transformed back into the trickster god and Loki landed nimbly on his feet. He spread the feathered cloak as wide as he could and bowed low, then stood and grinned with a gleam in his eye. "Congratulate me, my fellow gods."

None of the Norse gods said a word, all waiting patiently for news.

"Or not," Loki said, disappointed. He sighed. "Oh, well, I found your hammer, Thor. Thrym, Lord of Jotunheim, buried it eight leagues deep in the earth."

The younger Thor groaned. "Why?"

Loki shrugged, plopped himself down on a bench, and propped his feet up on a table. "He'll only give it back if Freya marries him."

The younger Thor nodded. "Right, then. Freya, get your veil!"

The goddess Freya glared at Thor coldly.

"What?" the thunder god protested. "You said you'd give anything you had to save my hammer!"

"And I would give anything I own!" the goddess protested. "But I won't marry Thrym!"

"B-but," the younger Thor sputtered. "But—"

Alex, sitting off to one side with the present-day Thor, laughed. "Way to smooth-talk the lady, big guy."

Thor's face darkened, but more with embarrassment than anger. "Well, our lives were at stake!"

Meanwhile, the younger Thor was protesting to his fellow gods. "Without my hammer, we'll be overrun with frost giants!"

Alex's Thor jabbed him in the chest with a finger as thick as an ax handle. "See. He knows."

Alex laughed again. "Yeah, that's two votes. You and you!"

Meanwhile, in the wyrd vision, Loki leaned back, tilting his bench over until it looked as if it would fall, but somehow managing to keep it perfectly balanced. And all the while he looked calm and confident. "You know . . . I might just have an idea. . . ."

Chapter Ten

The wyrd vision melted around them. For a moment, Alex and Thor, the spectators, seemed to stand nowhere. The walls, floor, and ceiling were all gray. In this brief space, Thor put one massive hand to his chin and shook his head. "I should have known better than to fall for this."

Alex was about to ask what "this" was, but a moment later he had his answer. The wyrd vision returned, and now Alex found himself on a rocky road. Up ahead, he could just make out the stone walls of a gigantic fortress. Looking closer, he saw the enormous backside of a figure dressed in a bridal gown walking with a much smaller figure dressed as a bridesmaid. Like the gods in the hall, these figures did not seem to notice Alex and Thor walking almost within arm's reach of them.

Suddenly, the gigantic bride stopped and turned toward the bridesmaid, throwing back a heavy veil to reveal Thor's even heavier beard. "The Mighty Thor is no man's bride!" he protested.

The bridesmaid too stopped, and Alex was not surprised at all to see that it was Loki in disguise. The mischievous god said, "Come on, Thor. We're only doing this to protect Asgard and the other gods. You're just pretending to be Freya until Thrym gives your hammer back."

The disguised Thor's face turned nearly purple. "He'll pay for making me do this."

The bridesmaid-Loki clicked his tongue and patted Thor on the arm. "Nonsense. You make a beautiful bride. I'd marry you myself. Of course," he added with a twinkle in his eye, "I'd be terrified to say no!"

The bride-Thor glared at Loki with murder in his eyes, but the present-day Thor laughed.

"He always got the better of me. I could never keep up when he started talking smart."

Alex looked up at the thunder god. "You didn't mind?"

Thor shrugged. "I liked him being smart. He liked me being strong. That's the way it is. Always was."

"Ah," Alex said. "Wyrd."

"Seemed normal to us," the thunder god said.

"Alex."

Alex heard Cleo's voice humming in his ear like a gnat. He had to smile to himself. Here he was, thinking it strange that Thor could transport them back in time. Meanwhile, *he* was able to talk to someone living in an entirely different reality.

"Yes?" he said as softly as possible.

"Mom's home. And I think she's got someone from the police department with her. I gotta go."

"But I'm going to need you!" Alex whispered.

There was no answer.

"Did you say something, Vali?" the present-day Thor asked.

"I said, uh, I wonder if they're going to feed you."

"Oh, they had a few snacks," Thor said discontentedly.

The wyrd vision melted and reformed once again. This time they were inside the fortress, standing at the edge of a feast given in the castle's courtyard. Tables stood in rows, and each of them looked ready to collapse under the weight of food piled as high as Alex's chin. There was enough food to feed an army, which was good because the master of the castle seemed to have invited one. Broad-shouldered warriors lined the benches, clutching and biting at hunks of meat and apples, fish and cranberries, and other food. More often than not, two men would grab for the same bit and fight for it. But instead of putting a stop to the brawls, the rest of the warriors simply laid hold of the fighters, tossed them off the benches, and moved into their seats.

Invisible Alex and Thor took up positions near the main table, where the "bride" and "bridesmaid" sat near a man in a heavy bronze crown who reclined in a thick-legged, skillfully carved chair. Alex knew this must be Thrym, the

King of Jotunheim. Beside him, the present-day Thor chuckled. "Watch. This is where it gets good."

Alex watched the younger Thor, still dressed as a bride. He hunched low over his platter of food like a wolf daring anyone to try to steal a bite. One hand swooped down and snatched a joint of meat and, lifting his veil a bit with the other hand, the thunder god began to tear at it with his teeth like a starving warrior.

Across the table, Thrym roared with laughter and pounded the table. "Look! Look! The gentle Freya eats like a man among us!"

Loki, still dressed as a bridesmaid, answered quickly and cleverly. "In her eagerness to come to my lord Thrym to be married, she did not stop to eat or drink for eight days on the road."

Off to one side, the real Thor tapped his forehead and winked at Alex. "You see? Smart."

"Well then, I won't keep the lady waiting!" Thrym roared. He clapped his hands. "You men! Bring Thor's hammer and put it in my bride's lap!"

Four of Thrym's warriors leaped to their feet and hurried out of the courtyard. Over the veil that hid his bearded face, Thor watched the men eagerly, and his stare did not go unnoticed by Thrym. "The gentle Freya's eyes," he said, "burn as brightly as a warrior's on the eve of battle."

Once again, Loki chimed in. "In her eagerness to reach you, she has not slept for eight nights on the road."

The King of Jotunheim laughed, and his men laughed with him.

The real Thor grinned and said in a soft rumble, "Ah, here comes the last laugh. . . ."

The four men returned, each holding one corner of a stretcher. In the middle of the stretcher lay the hammer of the thunder god. It was a simple-looking tool with a large stone head and a thick wooden handle. The four men staggered under its weight, sweating and gasping with the exertion it took to carry the hammer across the courtyard to where the "bride" sat.

"Behold the great hammer, Mjollner! It takes four men to carry that hammer!" Thrym said. "Only Thor can wield it barehanded."

"How right you are!" shouted the bride. The younger Thor suddenly leaped to his feet and threw off his disguise. "I am Thor!"

The god of thunder reached out and snatched

up the hammer with one hand as if it were a toy. The four men, suddenly relieved of the hammer's weight, staggered backward. Thor raised the hammer and brought it down on the feast table. The great oak table split in two with an ear-shattering crack. "This is my hammer!" the god roared. Next he turned to the chair in which he'd been sitting. One blow reduced the chair to splinters. "And you rest tonight with the dead in Helheim!"

The warriors scattered in sheer terror as Thor turned to Thrym himself. The King of Jotunheim sat in his chair, paralyzed with fear and amazement. "Nobody takes Thor's hammer," the god snarled.

He raised the hammer. Alex cried out and turned his eyes away as Thor brought the hammer down with a sickening crunch.

Chapter Eleven

Cleo had heard her mother's car pull up to the house. Wheeling herself to the window to make sure, she'd also seen a man get out of his car on the far side of the street and approach her mother as she walked to the front door. Cleo recognized Detective Saybrook, one of the officers who'd been investigating her father's disappearance. When he'd invited himself in and her mother had walked him to the kitchen, Cleo decided to do a little detective work of her own. As quietly as her chair could roll, she snuck up to the den that connected to the kitchen and waited. Someone standing on two legs might have been uncomfortable, shifted positions, and given themselves away with a noise. But Cleo sat just around the corner from her mother and the detective, as still and calm as a cat, and listened.

"... so you're finally reopening the case," her mother was saying. "I'm so glad. Now I hope you'll find him."

"I hope we will too, ma'am," said Detective Saybrook. "But I don't think you understand. This isn't a missing persons case anymore. It's a criminal investigation."

Cleo stifled a gasp of surprise, and she could almost hear her mother's jaw drop. "A ... a criminal," her mother stammered. Then she brought herself to say it. "With Matt as the suspect?"

Although Cleo couldn't see him, she imagined that Saybrook's face was calm and impassive. Someone speaking like that either enjoyed delivering bad news or hid his discomfort behind the plain and simple facts. Cleo found herself hoping it was the latter; if this Saybrook simply enjoyed his work, their father might be in real trouble.

Saybrook recited, "Something went missing the night he disappeared, ma'am. Apparently, that something could be worth a lot."

Mrs. Bellows's voice grew heavy with sadness and fatigue. "You don't know that."

"No, ma'am," the detective admitted. "And we won't know until we find your husband. But I do know that something was inside that statue. And whatever it was, it's now gone. And so is your husband."

Listening, Cleo heard a now familiar desperation in her mother's voice. "Something happened to my husband, Detective. He didn't sell off some ancient artifact and head for Aruba."

"I hope you're right," the detective said. But the tone of his voice sounded more like *I don't believe you.*

Mrs. Bellows's voice hardened. "I think you should leave."

There was a squeak of chairs as Detective Saybrook and her mother stood. Cleo silently rolled herself back a few feet, to make sure she stayed out of view. This time when he spoke, the policeman sounded genuinely sad. "I'm sorry about all this, Mrs. Bellows. It's just that I'm getting calls from the museum people. The captain's getting calls all the way from China. There's a lot of pressure on us to investigate and solve this thing. So we have to explore all the theories."

Mrs. Bellows thought about this for a moment. "And how many other theories are you considering?"

Detective Saybrook didn't answer.

"Like I said, I think you should leave," Cleo's mother insisted.

Cleo heard footsteps and the opening of the door, and then the police officer spoke again. "Does your husband speak Chinese?"

Her mother snapped. "He didn't go on a treasure hunt to China and forget to tell me!"

The door slammed.

Cleo braced herself and rolled into the hallway. Her mother would need her now—even if she shouldn't have been eavesdropping. In the entryway, she found her mother wiping a tear from her eye. Mother and daughter looked at each other; Cleo could see that her mother knew she'd heard the entire exchange.

"That," Mrs. Bellows sniffed, waving a hand dismissively at the departed policeman, "that wasn't anything you need to worry about—"

"This doesn't change anything," Cleo interrupted.

"What do you mean?"

Cleo spoke firmly, sounding a lot older than fifteen. "Statue or no statue, don't start thinking Dad ran out on us. You know that's not what happened."

Her mother sniffed again and looked away; this was a movement that, for as long as Cleo could remember, had meant she was crying. "I . . . I don't know what happened anymore." She sobbed. "Nobody knows."

"Mom . . ." Cleo felt tears well up in her eyes; in her heart, she wanted to tell her mother everything—about Gorgos, the computer, and Alex's adventures. But it would sound insane. Even when she and Alex talked about these adventures, these . . . mythquests, or whatever they were, they sounded unbelievable. How would they sound to a woman on the verge of a nervous breakdown? Cleo knew her mother needed something to cling to, but Cleo couldn't offer that. All she had was an unbelievable event connected to an impossible hope.

Finally, she said, "I . . . I've got to get back to my homework."

Chapter Twelve

The wyrd vision had ended. Alex found himself back in Thor's hall in midwinter. He listened to several more stories of Thor's adventures with Loki as the thunder god drained draft after draft of grog. Two things were very clear from the stories Thor told: first, that Loki was an immortal version of every class clown Alex had ever known—which meant that he was a funny guy until he was playing his jokes on *you*, and that, like the joker in every class, he sometimes pushed his games too far. The second was that, whatever Loki's faults, the other gods had accepted them.

But Alex wasn't really paying much attention to Thor's stories anymore. They were all the same after a while. Like television shows, they all had one formula: Loki caused a problem, then somehow convinced everyone that he could fix it, only to use this new opportunity to make things even worse, while none of the other gods seemed to catch on. The gods, who would apparently live forever, seemed destined to fall for the same tricks and believe the same lies over and over.

While Thor went on with yet another story of falling for Loki's trickery or smashing frost giants into icicles, Alex began to think about this concept of wyrd. From the moment his sister and Thor had explained it to him, Alex had felt an enormous weight lifted from his shoulders. Only now, in the security of Thor's hall, did Alex realize why. If everything that was to happen had already happened, then Alex bore no responsibility for finding his father. If his father was meant to be found, then Alex would find him. In fact, according to wyrd, Alex already *had* found him. Or, at least, he was destined to find him.

But what if it's not meant to be? Alex thought. *What if wyrd says I'll never find Dad?*

If the future was already set, then nothing Alex did could change it. If fate decreed that he would never find his father, then his quest was nothing but a waste of time. So there was a downside to wyrd as well.

A small voice, a tiny voice, faint but clear and full of guilt, whispered to him: *But at least you'll know it's not your fault.*

Instantly he regretted thinking it. *I won't accept that,* he told himself. *I don't care what sort of greater powers have decided I won't find my dad—I'm going to fight them. I'm going to win. And if that goes against fate, well then, that's someone else's problem.*

Across the table, Thor's head slumped down and he laid one cheek across his arm. He had downed enough grog to make even a thunder god tipsy.

"Of course," the god said, slurring his words, "Loki could go too far. Like that time he cut off all of Sif's hair in the middle of the night. But it was just a joke."

Alex raised an eyebrow. "That was a joke?"

"Sure," Thor said, his head still resting heavily on his arm. "We were like brothers. Sif was like a sister to him. Didn't you ever play jokes like that?"

Alex laughed. "Not yet."

"I'm back, and I heard that!"

Cleo's voice in his ear nearly made Alex jump out of his skin. "Geez, stop doing that! Everything okay?"

"I'm fine."

"Course," replied Thor, thinking the question had been directed at him. "I'm darely even brunk. Er . . . drunk. Everyone knows the thunder god can drain a horn with the best of them." To prove it, Thor sat up, his body waving this way and that unsteadily, and then downed another horn full of grog.

"There's no question," Alex admitted. "Refill?"

Thor thrust his horn out. Alex took it and walked over to a smaller table near the wall to fill the cup. As he did, he asked, "Mom okay?"

"I don't know. I don't think so. I'll tell you about it. Any sign of Dad while I was gone?"

"Zero. But if I ever have to write a report on practical jokes played on Norse gods, I've got it covered."

"Maybe you're wasting time there, Alex," Cleo observed.

"Maybe, but I don't have any brighter ideas. And by the way, in case you've forgotten, your idea of the bowl didn't work, and I don't exactly have a Plan B for getting home. So I'm going to keep working on this."

"Any progress?" his sister asked.

"I think we're about to find out."

Alex filled Thor's horn and carried both his and the thunder god's back to the table. Alex hadn't taken even a sip of his, but Thor thought that each time Alex went to the pitcher, he filled both horns.

"So," Alex said, "you and Loki were buds from way back."

Thor lifted his head long enough to wipe his chin and beard. "Hmmm. I really miss those times we went a-viking together."

"Biking?" Alex said, misunderstanding. He whispered to Cleo, "Did they go biking together?"

He heard Cleo laugh. "Now there's a mental

picture! No, he said 'a-viking.' It means adventuring. That's how the Vikings got their name."

"Right. I'll just store that away for good use when I write that paper," Alex said. To Thor, he decided to speak boldly. "So, what about letting Loki off the hook?"

Thor growled. But when he spoke, there was a hint of admiration in his voice. "Vali, you are always a good son to him. I remember how you stood by him when he nearly started that war between us and the frost giants. You love your father; you want to help him. That's why you're here."

"You have no idea how right you are," Alex replied.

"I miss Loki, too," the god of thunder admitted. "Things aren't the same around here."

"So there you go!" Alex said hopefully. "You're just giving a brother a hand."

"No." Thor's growl took on that low rumble that seemed to echo in the skies above them. "No, you weren't there, Vali. You didn't see what a terrible thing he did. He's not who he used to be. This wasn't just mischief. This was something else. What Loki did started a chain of events that are foretold in our prophecies. Because of Loki, it's the beginning of the end for the gods."

Chapter Thirteen

Once again, Alex experienced the magic of wyrd. Thor cast his gaze toward one of the polished shields on the wall, and Alex felt himself drawn into it. Once again, they moved through time, but not through space. When the mists of their vision cleared, Alex was still standing in Thor's hall. Once again, the cold winter had changed to high summer, but now it was nighttime. Torches hung from sconces on the walls, their sputtering flames lighting the huge room until not a single shadow hid in a corner.

The Great Hall was crowded with the Norse gods, all of them laughing and drinking and eating. Now and then a voice rose in a coarse, loud song, then subsided, laughing, into the jumble of other voices. Horns of grog were slammed together in brash toasts; men slapped one another on the back or challenged each other to wrestling matches and fell tumbling over the tables. They were acting, Alex thought, exactly as he'd expect Vikings to act.

In the corner from which he watched the feast, Alex could feel the present-day Thor's presence. Unlike their earlier trip, when Thor had been excited and amused by Loki's pranks, this time the thunder god stood there as tensed as a coiled spring. His face was dark and his eyes flicked here and there, as though he was looking for some clue to preventing a catastrophe.

"Well, they seem to be having a good time," Alex said.

"Wait," Thor growled, "and watch."

As the vision swirled around them, Alex caught sight of the younger Thor. He was standing at one end of the hall, throwing his head back and laughing loudly enough to shake the mountain to its base. Beside him stood another god, a man with an incredibly handsome face. If Alex had seen a guy that good-looking on the school campus, he would have instantly assumed that the newcomer was a stuck-up jerk. But, aside from being handsome, this god also appeared innocent and completely unself-conscious. Even from a distance, Alex knew instantly that this being was nearly perfect—brave, kindhearted, and gentle.

"Balder," Thor said, his voice filled with sadness.

In the vision, Thor pushed Balder until he stood next to a wall. Then the thunder god stopped a dozen paces away, turned, and lifted his hammer from his belt. "All right, clear the way! It's my turn!"

When the other gods saw what Thor intended to do, they scattered, leaving a wide aisle down the center of the hall. At the far end of that aisle stood Balder, flashing a friendly and confident smile.

"Oh, no," Alex said, "don't tell me he's going to—"

Thor hurled his hammer. The mighty weapon flew through the air, breaking the sound barrier and filling the hall with a sonic boom.

Plates rattled and tables jumped a foot into the air. The gods themselves stumbled back from the sheer force of the hammer as it flew across the room. Alex had only the briefest moment to feel horror at the thought of that missile punching through Balder's chest before the hammer struck. . . .

To Alex's shock, the hammer simply bounced off Balder and fell to the floor with a dull thud.

The assembled gods let out a raucous cheer, hooting and clapping Balder on the back one by one. Even Thor laughed. "Another round of mead!"

"Now me!" chuckled Heimdall, dressed all in white just as he had been when Alex met him at the Rainbow Bridge. Heimdall hoisted a long javelin with a sharp, gleaming tip. Balder grinned and puffed out his chest again, but Thor scoffed. "If my hammer Mjollner can't harm him, nothing can harm him!"

Heimdall took aim anyway. He paced forward two or three steps and let the javelin fly. Its speed nearly rivaled the hammer's, and the result was the same. The spear simply bounced off the handsome god's chest. Heimdall loosed a howl of pleasure. "Now every god has tried his hand and still Balder stands. Untouched." The guardian of the Rainbow Bridge scooped up a massive tankard of mead and raised it toward Balder. "To Balder the Beautiful!"

"To Balder the Beautiful!" echoed the other Norse gods.

Alex looked up at the real Thor, the one watching with him. This Thor too raised his drink, but his face was clouded and his shoulders were heavy with sadness. "To Balder," he whispered in a voice thick with grief.

"What happens next?" Alex asked.

"Watch," Thor said. "But I warn you, you will not like it."

Alex turned back to the scene in Thor's hall, searching for something wrong—for the object that filled even the mighty thunder god with dread. At first he saw only the smiling faces of the Norse gods. Their heads were often thrown back in laughter, their arms waving wildly as they danced or gestured or arm wrestled each other, sometimes shoving aside entire platters of food to make room for a match. Except for the damage to the furniture, Alex could see nothing wrong.

Then his eyes fell on Loki. The slim, sharp-eyed god stood in a corner, and Alex realized that Loki had not moved a muscle. Of all the gods, he was the only one who had not raised a toast to Balder. He was so still, half hidden in the shadows, that Alex might have thought he was asleep, except that his keen eyes continually scanned the room. After a moment, those eyes settled on one of the Norse gods, a god in brown furs who stood a little apart from the rest of the party. This figure had eye sockets filled only with milky whiteness, and Alex knew immediately that the god was blind.

Loki detached himself from the wall and slid through the crowd, sidling up to the blind god.

"Good afternoon, Hoder," said Loki.

Hoder half-turned, directing all his remaining senses toward the newcomer. "Loki, is it? I know that voice. The last time I heard that voice, I believe you were trying to sell me an old cow you said was a young bull."

"But you were too wise for me, with eyes or without," Loki admitted. "And speaking of wisdom, surely even a blind god like you can see that not every god has tried his hand against Balder's strength."

Heimdall, who had passed by to refill his goblet, overheard Loki and chimed in. "Nothing harms him. Knives don't cut him. Spears don't pierce him. Rocks shatter or fall short."

Hoder, the blind god, nodded. "The enchantment that Frigga laid on him is amazing."

Loki studied Hoder, who of course could not return his stare. "Tell me, Hoder," Loki asked innocently, "what did you throw?"

Hoder laughed. "Me? I'm not a warrior. I'm blind."

"But Heimdall said all the gods," Loki remarked casually.

Hoder merely shrugged. "What is your point, Loki?"

"Why, nothing at all, my dear Hoder. Just making an observation. Now, if you'll excuse me."

A smile spread across Loki's face, but it was a smile that sent a chill down Alex's spine. The trickster god sidled away from Hoder and glided smoothly toward the door, lifting a cloak from a peg on the wall and wrapping it around himself as he slipped out. Curious, Alex followed him.

Chapter Fourteen

Perhaps it was the magic of the wyrd vision, or maybe it was some other magic in the realm of Asgard, but the moment Alex stepped out of Thor's hall, he found himself arriving instantly at his destination. He suddenly stepped into a beautiful garden, with a hundred types and sizes of flowers blooming all around him, their colors shining even at night. Foxgloves and snapdragons, lilacs and lilies filled the air with their scent. Into this garden Loki slithered like a snake.

But as Alex watched, Loki seemed to change shape. He pulled the cloak more tightly about him and hunched his shoulders. His body seemed to shrink in on itself, and his back bent as though under a heavy load. His pace slowed to a limp. His face, which had disappeared into the folds of his cloak for a moment, reappeared now, but his nose had grown long and crooked, framed by wiry white hair. He had become an old woman.

As Loki entered the garden at one end, a goddess appeared at the other. Like the other Norse gods, she looked youthful, but not quite as young as the others. She had about her the air of motherhood. Alex recognized her as Frigga, the queen of the Norse gods.

"Forgive me, my lady," said Loki in the high, scratchy voice of an old crone. "But is that your hall there?" She pointed beyond the garden to a handsome building with a roof that shone like silver in the moonlight.

Frigga smiled. "No, but my sons live there."

The old woman cackled to herself. "Yes, yes, yes, I saw them playing there. A strange sort of game it was."

"What do you mean?" asked Frigga.

The old woman raised one crooked finger to her chin. "One of them was stripped to the waist, and the others threw weapons. Swords and spears and rocks, as though to kill him. All the while laughing and drinking."

"Sounds like a party in some rough neighborhoods I know," Alex whispered.

Frigga put a gentle hand on the old woman's shoulder. "Don't worry, grandmother. That's my son Balder, most beautiful of the gods. He is safe."

"Safe! Safe!" croaked the old woman. "When the other gods hurl weapons at him?"

The queen of the Norse gods smiled. "Nothing can harm Balder. I was afraid for him, so I went through the world, asking everything to promise never to hurt him."

The old woman raised an eyebrow into her wrinkled forehead. "Everything in the world? Everything?"

Frigga nodded. "Water, so he can't drown. Fire, so he can't burn. Wood and stone and iron, so no weapon made in the nine worlds can kill him."

Alex heard Cleo whisper in his ear. "That is so Mom!"

The old woman looked doubtful. "You asked the rivers?"

"Every one."

"And the oceans?" the old woman added.

"And the mountains, and the sky."

The old woman shook her head. "Oak and ash and pine?"

Frigga opened her arms wide, displaying the vibrant plants in her garden. "And rhubarb and ivy. Everything that grows on the earth or under it."

The old woman reached over and plucked a sprig of leaves from a tiny vine. "And this mistletoe?"

Frigga laughed aloud. "This is too small a thing to worry about." Still laughing, the queen of the gods turned away in a swirl of elegant robes and walked back through her garden.

"And still," whispered the old woman to herself, "out of small things great problems may grow." Then she too turned and left the garden, the mistletoe still in her hand.

The world swirled about Alex, and instantly he was transported back to Thor's hall and the game of the gods. The party was still in full swing, with servants carrying in more platters of meat and new tankards of grog. One of the revelers snatched an iron tankard off a serving tray and hurled it at Balder. The handsome god easily snatched the tankard out of the air and took a long swig.

"Well done!" someone roared.

"Yes, well done indeed."

It was Loki's voice, oily and slick. The trickster god had returned to the hall, having slipped out of his old woman disguise. He now stood next to Hoder.

"Watch this," the present-day Thor growled under his breath. "Watch this and tell me he's my brother. Tell me what happened to the Loki I used to know."

Loki turned toward Hoder with a charming smile. "It's your turn to the play the game, my friend."

Hoder shook his head. "You're a fool. I can't see to play."

"But what are friends for? I'll guide your arm." Loki raised his voice above the laughter and noise of the Norse gods. "Let us see what Hoder can do!"

The din of the feast slowly died down as more and more of the Norse gods realized what Loki had asked. Most thought he was joking, but as he stood there waiting for them to respond, many of the gods moved forward curiously.

One of them was the younger Thor. "A blind man?" the thunder god asked. "What is his weapon?"

Loki proudly held up a tiny arrow, not much more than a dart, made of wood. "This."

The Norse gods erupted in laughter again. Heimdall slapped his knee. "That tiny thing? Spears and swords haven't harmed him. What will that thorn do?"

The present-day Thor, standing beside Alex, moaned, "That's what we all thought. Even Balder."

But Loki bore all their laughter and joking with immense patience, the smile never fading from his lips. "Let Hoder have his turn, and we'll see," he said.

The Norse gods grumbled but slowly gave way, clearing a path between Balder and the blind god Hoder.

"Hey," Alex said. "Hey, they're taking him seriously."

"Yes, we did," the present-day Thor said.

"But we've got to stop it," Alex protested. Thor didn't move.

In the vision, Balder stood as straight and proud as an elm tree. He smiled as Loki positioned Hoder in front of him and raised the blind god's arm.

"No," Alex said.

"Alex!" Cleo shouted from the real world. "This is bad! Do something!"

"No!" Alex shouted at the top of his lungs.

"Vali!" Thor called out to him. "Don't bother. You can't change the past."

Alex ignored him. He ran forward, dodging left and right to avoid the gods standing in his way. As he did, he heard Heimdall say, "Let me see that toy!"

Just as Alex reached Loki, the trickster god tossed the little dart to Heimdall.

"No, give it to me!" Alex demanded. No one responded. No one even heard him.

Heimdall caught the twig in midair and spun it around his finger. "Why, my fingernails get sharper than this!"

Alex ran over to Heimdall. "Don't let him do it!"

"Let me see that!" boomed the wyrd-Thor. Heimdall tossed the mistletoe right over Alex's head to the thunder god. Alex jumped but missed the dart by inches. He landed and slipped in grog, banging his knees on the ground and stumbling against a table covered in empty goblets. The goblets clattered noisily to the ground, followed by a big serving tray.

"I couldn't even pick my teeth with this!" laughed the Thor from the past. The crowd roared again, and the thunder god tossed the mistletoe back to Loki.

"Well then," the crafty god said, "it'll be a little time lost on a losing affair. Come, Hoder."

"Alex!" Cleo called out.

Alex looked down at the goblets and tray. If he had knocked them over, then maybe he could affect the past. He snatched up the tray and ran over to Balder.

The handsome god stood there, a confident smile on his face as Hoder, at Loki's urging, took the dart and threw his hand forward. The tiny dart—little more than a gnat compared to the thunder and lightning of Thor's hammer and Heimdall's spear—seemed to drift across the space between them, almost purposeless in its flight.

Alex stood there, holding the big tray out in midair, right in the dart's path. He watched the dart sail toward him, straight to the center of his makeshift shield . . . and then pass through it as though it didn't exist.

"No!" he yelled. He spun around in time to watch the dart land squarely in the center of Balder's chest, just above his heart.

The other gods were still laughing, but Balder suddenly glanced down at his chest, a curious look crossing his handsome face. His face turned ashen gray and, an instant later, the great god toppled to his knees, then fell on his face.

The moment seemed frozen in time: the Norse gods staring in disbelief, Loki's mischievously grinning face the only one in the room that did not express sheer horror, and Balder's body lifeless on the floor. Then, with painful slowness, the color drained from the scene and it faded away like an afterimage. Alex found himself back in Thor's hall, gray with winter.

Thor poured another draft of mead down his throat. The thunder god looked unsteady on his feet, though from grog or grief Alex could not say.

"I told you," Thor said darkly. "You cannot

change the past. Don't you think I'd have changed it if I could? I'd give my strong right arm to change that hour!"

"That was . . ." Alex paused, searching for the right word. "That was terrible. How could he have done that?"

The god rested his chin on his barrel chest for a moment, then lifted it to look fiercely at Alex. "That's your father, Vali! The one who killed the best of us with a trick!"

Alex backed away from the sheer force of Thor's anger. Now that he'd seen what Loki had done, it was hard to feel sympathy for the trickster. "I didn't know."

The thunder god sat down heavily on a bench. He was still talking, but his words were thick and drowsy. "I won't help you free him, Vali. No god will."

Leaning forward, Thor folded his enormous arms on the table and rested his head in the pillow of his hands. A moment later he was fast asleep and snoring loudly.

Cleo piped up. "Nice work, Alex. You just got a Norse god dead drunk."

At the table, Thor groaned in his sleep.

"Now what?" Cleo asked.

Alex tried to gather some courage. "Now I make my big mistake."

"What do you mean?" Cleo asked.

Alex walked over to Thor's hammer. Although it had looked a normal size in Thor's hand, as Alex drew near to it he realized that it was almost the size of a sledgehammer. Still, how heavy could it be? Alex wrapped his hands around the handle, braced himself, and lifted.

The hammer didn't budge. In fact, it didn't shift the slightest bit. Alex might as well have wrapped his hands around a mountain.

"Give it up, Alex. No one but Thor can lift it," Cleo said.

"Unless I'm wearing those." Alex pointed to Thor's belt. The two gloves were still tucked there. "They're supposed to be magic, right? I can lift the hammer if I wear them."

"Alex, no! You think those gloves are going to protect you from Thor? Do you have any idea what Thor did to the last guy who stole his hammer?"

Alex gulped. "I saw."

He tiptoed forward and put his hands on the gloves. They were made of thick leather, and they were soft and pliable. But they weren't easy to remove. Alex tugged once. They slipped partway out, then got caught in the thunder god's belt.

Thor snorted and mumbled something to himself.

"This is nuts, Alex! Loki is not one of the good guys. He's not worth this!"

"You're not wrong," Alex whispered, desperate not to wake Thor. "But the guy's tied to a rock with a poisonous snake over his head." He tugged again, but the gloves still wouldn't budge. "I'd like to call in Amnesty International, but this is out of their jurisdiction. So I guess that means it's up to me."

The sleeping god snorted and shifted. Alex jerked his hands back, away from the gloves, and waited. Only when Thor had completely resettled into a drunken sleep did he try again. This time he changed tactics. Instead of tugging at the gloves, he grabbed hold of them and pulled with one clean jerk. The gloves slid free. Thor snorted and slapped a hand to his thigh as if squashing a bug, then fell back into a deep sleep.

"Got 'em!" Alex said.

Chapter Fifteen

The moment he slipped the gloves on, Alex felt a surge of strength like a superhero who had just discovered his secret powers. With gloves like these in the real world, Alex could probably lift a car off its tires. Of course, in the real world, these gloves wouldn't even exist.

Alex wrapped his gloved hands around the hammer again and heaved it up. This time the hammer left the table and he was able to bring it up to his shoulder, although it felt as if it weighed a thousand pounds. Alex held it in both hands, with the handle leaning against his shoulder, trying to keep his feet beneath him as he staggered out of Thor's hall and down the steep mountainside.

"Well," he said, looking down the narrow trail toward the bottom. "With this hammer, if I slip, it's going to be a very fast ride to the bottom."

He wound his way carefully down the steep trail, pasing once again through layers of cloudy sky, past the aeries of eagles, and into the foothills until he came to the bottom of Thor's mountain.

"Listen," Cleo said to him. She'd been quiet for some time. "I've been reading, and we have a problem. You can't do this."

"It's the only way to free Loki," Alex insisted. Shifting the heavy hammer to his other shoulder, he started toward Loki's cave.

"That's the problem," Cleo insisted. "It's—"

Her words were drowned out by the sound of thunder and the shock of a lightning bolt striking the ground at Alex's feet. He staggered backward. "Oh, great. Thor's up."

Gripping the hammer tightly, Alex put his head down and ran.

If Alex had had time to think about it, he

would have laughed at how impossible it was: he had just stolen a mystical hammer from the Norse god of thunder, and now he was sprinting across a stony wasteland, dodging bolts of lightning as they rained down from the sky.

And they did fall like rain. Bolt after jagged bolt streaked downward, sizzling through the air to pound the rocks that surrounded him. Some landed just in front, while others scorched the ground behind him, where he had stepped just a moment before. As he ran, Alex had the distinct and terrifying feeling that Thor was zeroing in on him.

"Alex," Cleo called out. "Listen to me. . . ."

"Not now!" he yelled.

Crack! Another bolt struck, close enough that Alex felt heat and electricity sting his heels.

"Alex!"

Crack!

"Not now!" He saw the icy cold pool before him and knew that the cave must be close.

"You-cannot-free-Loki!" In any other situation, the sheer force of Cleo's voice might have stopped Alex in his tracks. But compared to the thunderbolts that were crashing down on him, Cleo's shout barely touched him.

"I think I can," he gasped back, reaching the icy pool.

"No, you can't. You shouldn't!"

Crack!

"I . . . can't really . . . have this conversation right now," Alex panted, struggling to keep the hammer on his shoulder. "Got a thunder god on my heels."

"Thor is not the problem."

"Maybe not for you!"

Crack! A lightning bolt struck dead in the middle of the pool, sending up a spout of water that seemed to be on fire. Alex ran through a shower, then sprinted the last dozen yards to the cave he'd visited before. Once he was inside, shielded from the lightning bolts, he stumbled to his knees to rest, letting the hammer hit the ground with a thud that made the rocky walls shiver.

"Okay," he gasped. "Now talk."

Cleo spoke with great urgency. "I've been tracking Loki through every Norse legend I can find. In every single version, after the Norse gods bound Loki, he stayed bound."

"Yeah, but that's just wrong," Alex protested. The lightning storm continued, with bolt after bolt blasting the rocks at the edge of the cave. But none of them seemed able to get inside. "Besides, that's the point. Gorgos talked about breaking the myth so we could get out."

"You saw what Loki did," Cleo argued back. "He killed Balder. That's why he's there."

Alex laid his head back against the cool wall of the cave. Doubt began to gnaw at him. "I know, I know. The guy's not exactly Nobel Peace Prize material. I get that."

"So why are you doing this?" Cleo demanded.

Alex bit his lip. He knew why he was doing it. In his heart, he knew. And it had nothing to do with Loki. He blurted out, "Because I can't just write him off! Yes, he did something terrible—does that mean he's not worth caring about? What if he regrets his choice now?"

For a moment, there was silence. Even the thunder seemed to have stopped. The silence reached from the Alterworld to the real world, from Loki's cave to Dr. Bellows's den, as brother and sister shared a single thought: their father was worth caring about. He would not be written off.

Alex heard Cleo sigh and finally whisper, "I'm not saying you shouldn't care about Loki. But that doesn't mean you should set him loose."

Alex said nothing. Cleo continued. "The only mentions of Loki getting free are in the descriptions of Ragnarok."

"Ragna-what?" Alex asked.

"Ragnarok. The end of the world. According to Norse mythology, if you let Loki go, the whole world will be destroyed."

"Oh, well that's just ridicul—" Alex paused. "You found a story where Vali frees his father?"

"No, no, Vali doesn't free his father. That doesn't happen in any of the stories."

"Then you don't know what would happen if he did."

Cleo's voice grew tense. "We're talking end of the world, Alex. Are you going to take the chance?"

Alex let his head slump forward, catching it in his hands and rubbing his temples. He hadn't asked for any of this. He had never intended to get sucked into some myth world in the first place, and he had certainly never wanted to return. All he wanted was to get his father back. He didn't want to fulfill any Norse mythology. He certainly didn't want to get fried by lightning bolts. He had never asked to play by their rules, and he didn't care if the entire place was wiped off the face of . . . the face of wherever he was.

"Alex—?"

"Yes," he said, finally answering. "I'm going to take the chance."

Chapter Sixteen

In the den of the Bellows house, Cleo watched the story unfold on the computer screen before her. She watched her brother struggle into the cave, carrying the hammer two-handed. All was as it had been before, with Loki chained to the rocks and his wife, Sigyn, standing over him, catching the snake's venom in a stone bowl.

As he entered, Sigyn turned to him in surprise and delight. "You did it!"

Loki lifted his head and looked both pleased

and dismayed. "You took Thor's hammer? You could have been killed!"

Sigyn turned to Loki. "He did it for you."

Cleo leaned close to the microphone that carried voice commands into the computer and shouted, "Alex, don't do it!" She saw him flinch. "Loki doesn't get free until the gods have their final battle. They all kill each other and they destroy the world. If you break those chains, that happens now!"

Alex raised the hammer over his head. "That's your theory," he replied.

He brought Mjollner down. The massive stone head struck the chains that lay across a rock with a loud *boom*. Sparks flew.

Lying across the rocks, Loki let loose a wail that was both pain and joy. "At last!" he howled. "At last I'll be free!"

Venom dripped from the snake's fangs above, splashing on Loki's face. His cry of triumph turned to a scream of pain. Cleo glanced over at a second computer screen—the screen of the laptop on which she'd done her Norse research. File after file had repeated the same information.

"That's how it is, Alex," she insisted. "That's how that world works. It's wyrd, remember? Things happen the way they always happened."

Cleo saw her brother set his jaw in the same look of determination she'd seen her entire life. "Not this time."

He brought the hammer down a second time. More sparks flew, but as they cleared, Cleo could see that the chain had cracked.

In that same moment, Cleo felt a tremor through the wheels of her chair. The chair rolled backward slightly. Then she realized that the walls were shaking.

"Alex . . . ," she said, not sure what she was going to tell him.

On the screen, Loki looked up at Alex, pleading with him. "Do it, Vali. Please!"

Alex gathered his strength and attacked the chains, striking once, twice, three more times.

Behind Alex, Sigyn leaned forward, her voice growing more passionate. "Yes, yes! Free your father!"

But Cleo could hardly pay attention. The tremors she had felt grew. In the way of earthquakes, their strength multiplied rapidly—one moment there was a gentle rumble and sway, and the next it felt as if a giant had grabbed hold of the house and was shaking it violently. Books flew from the shelves and landed on the floor in chaotic piles.

Alex struck the chains again.

Downstairs in the Bellows house, Lily Bellows grabbed hold of the door frame to keep her balance as the earthquake died down, then returned with renewed force. A stack of plates slid off the counter and crashed to the floor.

In the Alterworld, Alex raised Mjollner again and slammed it down on the crack in the chains.

In the real world, miles from the Bellows house at the university, Barbara Frazier was thrown off her feet by the force of the earthquake. Every artifact on her shelf rattled, threatening to come crashing down on her.

The frosted glass of Matt's office door cracked, the crack running right through his first name.

Alex raised the hammer again.

In the Bellowses' den, Cleo wheeled herself back to the microphone. "Alex, stop! Stop! We're having an earthquake. Out here!"

Alex hesitated. The hammer hovered over

his head, wavering. The gloves gave him strength, but barely enough to hold the hammer up so high. He heard Cleo's voice: "You have to leave him there. Or it's the end of the world. And not just in there!"

Suddenly Sigyn stepped forward, urging him. "Hurry, Alex! Hurry! Do it now!" It was the Gorgos voice, the voice Alex hadn't heard before.

Alex froze. Suddenly, the hammer lost its weight. The chains around Loki lost their meaning. He had just heard something impossible.

In the real world, Cleo had heard it too, and suddenly she knew the woman wasn't really Sigyn. "Gorgos!" she gasped.

Alex lowered the hammer to his shoulder and turned toward Sigyn. The figure before him was still that of a Norse goddess, but something had changed. Her face was no longer shadowed and mysterious, no longer filled with the sadness of a woman who would spend eternity tending to her tormented husband. Sigyn's face was now filled with an evil mischief of its own. The grin on her face was suddenly familiar to him. It was the grin he'd seen at the edge of the Minotaur's labyrinth— the same grin he'd seen in the shield at Thor's hall.

"It's you again!" he said. "Gorgos!"

Sigyn, or Gorgos, chuckled.

"Where's my father?" Alex demanded.

The creature motioned to Loki and asked in that eerie voice, "How do you know that's not your father?"

Alex's heart skipped a beat. He glanced at Loki. "D-Dad? Is that you?"

Loki, exhausted from pain, rasped, "Son..."

"It's me, Alex," he said. "Alex!"

"Help...me," Loki pleaded.

"Go on, *son*," Gorgos taunted. "Help him."

Alex felt his fingers gripping the hammer tightly. He was sure that inside the gauntlets his fingers had gone white. The chained god before him looked wretched and tormented. But that same cold dread had filled Alex upon seeing Gorgos...a dread that crept up his spine to tickle his neck with icy fingers.

"No," he said at last. He looked at the creature with the face of Sigyn. "No. I don't know what you're up to, but I'm not helping you anymore." He looked back at Loki. "I'm sorry."

Alex dropped the hammer.

In the Bellows house, Cleo felt the tremors

123

subside. The windows stopped rattling and the floor grew still. The earthquake had ended.

But in the Alterworld, the cave walls shook with a new sound, a booming voice that thundered down the tunnel. *"Vali! Where's my hammer?"*

Chapter Seventeen

Thor stormed into the cave, large and fast as a hurricane. Before Alex could react, the god reached out and grabbed him by the neck, lifting him off the ground. "That is my hammer!" he roared.

The hammer fell from Alex's hand as Thor slammed him up against the cave wall. The god's thick-fingered hand squeezed his windpipe, and Alex gasped for air.

"Alex!" Cleo cried out in alarm.

Alex kicked and clawed, but he was no match for the god of thunder. Thor's face was red. Veins throbbed in his forehead.

"Thor! Thor, stop!"

The voice was small, weak, and desperate enough to make the thunder god ease his grip. Thor turned to see Loki struggling weakly in his chains, craning his neck to look around. Loki pleaded, "Please, please. I already paid with one son's life. Don't take the other."

Thor loosened his grip further, but then Sigyn glided forward, hissing in her normal voice, "He's not your son!" She pointed at Alex. "He's not Vali!"

Thor glanced first at Sigyn, then at Alex. His brow furrowed in concentration. "What are you?"

Alex could still barely breathe, but he managed to blurt out, "My father . . . my father is in trouble too."

Loki moaned, "He tried to help. Let him go."

Thor hesitated a moment, then made his decision. He released Alex, letting him drop to the floor of the cave. Then he gently scooped up the hammer and spun it around in his hand. The moment Mjollner was back in his hands, the anger drained from his face. He turned to Alex and said simply, "Give me my gloves."

Alex hastily pulled them off his hands and held them out. Thor snatched them away and tucked them back into his belt.

Alex climbed to his feet, rubbing his throat and coughing. He tried to speak but choked, then coughed again. All the while he staggered toward Sigyn, and when he was finally able to speak, he said accusingly, "You tried to trick me."

Gorgos sneered. "Trick you? You were more than halfway to your choice before I ever helped. You wanted to save Loki even before I gave you a little extra reason." A look of disdain spread over the creature's face. "Tell me, why'd you want to help a murderer? Did you think if you helped Loki, some other sucker would help your father?"

Alex did not back down. "I helped him because you asked me to. You wanted this."

Sigyn, or Gorgos, opened her mouth to speak, but at that moment another drop of venom spilled onto Loki's face. He screamed in agony, and the ground shook again. Alex rushed to the chained god's side. Beside the rocks, he spotted the stone bowl Sigyn had used to catch the venom.

"You've got to—" he started to say, but the Sigyn creature had vanished.

Another drop of venom fell, and another acid splash seared Loki's face. With every cry, a tremor shook the Alterworld.

"I have to do something!" he said desperately.

"You can't free him," Cleo said firmly.

"I know. I'm not going to. But I have to do something. Where's her bowl?"

He saw it at his feet and bent to pick it up. As he did, he noticed a small carving on the side of the stone bowl—a serpent, painted green. "Hey, this looks familiar—" he started to say. The moment he touched the bowl, the entire world shifted around him. The cave, Loki, and Thor all melted away in an instant, and Alex found himself back in his father's study with Cleo smiling at him.

"You're back!" Cleo said. She wheeled toward him and gave him a big hug around the middle. "You got back!"

But Alex was still too stunned by what he'd seen. The transition was too overwhelming. He thought of Loki. "He saved me."

Cleo nodded. "He loved his son."

Epilogue

Alex sat on the edge of the weight bench at the clinic, watching his sister do arm curls with free weights. He played around with the bench press for a minute, but he was feeling completely unmotivated to work out.

Cleo rolled a five-pound weight up to her shoulder and down. "I hope you learned your lesson."

Alex grunted. "What lesson? Not to feel sorry for someone?"

"No!" Cleo put down her weights and spun

to face her brother directly. She felt awkward expressing her feelings, but the truth was that these were awkward times. She continued, "I like that you cared about Loki and wanted to help him. That's one of the great things about you." She paused. "But just because you feel bad for a guy in prison doesn't mean he should be set free."

Alex thought about that for a moment, deciding that she was right, at least in Loki's case. But he would never feel totally happy about it. No matter what his reasons, he had still left the god behind to be tormented forever.

"Do you think," he asked finally, "that it really would have happened? The end of the world, I mean?"

Cleo shrugged. "I think we were about two hammer blows away from finding out. We're messing with some major stuff here."

"You want us to stop?" Alex asked.

Cleo pondered that for a moment. It was like lifting weights, she decided, only much more important. She had to keep going if she wanted results. "No," she said. "I want us to be more careful. I want you to stop and listen to me sometimes."

Alex stood up. "You're out here with the

books. It's different when you're there, believe me. You can't not get involved. The stories don't feel like stories. It's real. The people are *real*."

Cleo nodded. "I'm sure you're right. That's why we have to work as a team, okay? It's the only way to make sure we get Dad back."

For a moment, Alex looked as if he would get angry. But there was nothing for him to be angry about—Cleo was right. He had nearly caused the end of the world. If he had listened to her, it wouldn't have happened.

"Deal," he said a little sharply. But he flashed her a smile as he left the room.

Cleo watched him go. She knew he would be all right. He just needed to blow off some steam. She couldn't expect him to get zapped into an alien world, look for their missing father, and then come back as happy as a lark when he failed. He had only visited the Alterworld twice, and already he'd been attacked by a Minotaur and nearly fried by lightning from a thunder god. He had a right to be edgy.

But she also knew he would go back. Neither one of them would give up on their father. He was in there somewhere, and they wouldn't rest until he was safe. Besides, she couldn't help wondering about the word *real,* which Alex had used. "How real is real? Is Loki still in there, chained in that cave? Or does it all disappear when we turn it off? What would have happened if we'd set him free? Ragnarok? The end of the *world*?"

THOR'S HAMMER AND
LOKI'S PUNISHMENT

Hammer of the Gods presents two distinct
Norse myths woven together. Norse gods were a
rough-and-tumble group who were immortal
but not perfect. Thor was strong and powerful,
honest and brave, but his wits were not as sharp
as those of many others. Loki, though physically
weak and cowardly, was very intelligent and fond
of using his cleverness to cause trouble.

Every day Thor woke and reached for
Mjollner, his mighty hammer. This weapon was
so heavy that none but Thor could lift it without

special gloves. Thor used the hammer to protect Asgard, the home of the gods, from danger. One morning the hammer was not there. Thor searched every corner of Asgard but could not find it. Finally he approached Loki, who was not known for his trustworthiness.

Loki swore that he'd had nothing to do with the theft, and Thor was satisfied that he was telling the truth. After all, no coward could lie in the face of Thor's wrath. But where was Thor's hammer? At last Loki had an idea. He went to the goddess Freya and borrowed a magical feather cloak that enabled him to fly. He traveled all around the world until he finally came to the land of the giants, where he encountered the giants' king.

"I've taken Thor's hammer," the king confessed, "and I won't give it back unless beautiful Freya marries me."

Lori flew back to Asgard and told Thor the news. Thor went directly to Freya, who absolutely refused to marry Thrym, the stupid, ugly king of the giants.

The gods convened a council to resolve this problem. Without Thor's hammer, they had no protection against the giants. In many versions of this story, not Loki but Heimdall, the guardian of the Rainbow Bridge that connected Asgard to the earth, came up with the plan to disguise Thor as Freya. Thor was not enthusiastic, but Loki liked the plan—and the idea of seeing the strongest god in a dress—and he used all his cunning to persuade Thor. But Loki did have to agree to travel along as a bridesmaid.

When they arrived at Thrym's palace, there was a great feast. Thor refused to speak, and Loki explained that the bride was hoarse from her screams of joy at her upcoming wedding. Thor ate like a warrior, not a blushing bride, and Loki explained that the bride hadn't eaten in days because she was so excited about her marriage. Later Thrym lifted Thor's veil and was shocked by Thor's fierce eyes, and Loki explained that the bride was so eager to meet her new husband that she hadn't slept in days.

Though Thrym wanted the wedding to proceed immediately, Loki insisted he produce the hammer first, so the giant laid the great hammer on his bride's lap. Thor grabbed the hammer and made quick work of the giants. Together he and Loki traveled back to Asgard in great delight over their adventure.

Loki's adventures didn't always work out so well. He was fiercely jealous of Balder, the most beloved of all the gods. Every living creature loved Balder for his goodness. But an early death had been prophesied for Balder, so Frigga, his mother, went to every living creature and asked each one not to harm her son. With this protection, Balder became invincible, and the gods took great pleasure in the game of throwing things at him, causing no harm at all.

Loki hated seeing the joy Balder brought to the other gods, and one day he disguised himself as an old woman and went to visit Frigga. They discussed the game of the gods. Frigga explained that nothing would hurt her son. When Loki-in-disguise asked if all the creatures had given Frigga their promise, the goddess said that there was one little mistletoe bush she hadn't bothered to ask, since it was so small. Loki immediately picked some mistletoe and carried it back to the gods.

Balder had a brother named Hoder who was blind. Hoder never played the gods' game because he had no weapon. Loki coaxed Hoder to join the others and gave him a twig to toss. Hoder did as Loki suggested and threw the mistletoe. The dart struck Balder and killed him instantly.

The gods were so upset by Balder's death that they hunted Loki, who made himself scarce. They turned Loki's son Vali into a wolf, which immediately devoured his brother, Narvi. But Loki's pain was only beginning. The gods made chains of Narvi's entrails and shackled Loki to a rock. Above him they placed a serpent that dripped venom on the god. Though Sigyn, Loki's wife, positioned herself above Loki to catch the poison, she regularly had to empty her bowl, and then the venom dripped onto Loki and caused him great pain. Some say that when he feels pain, he screams so loudly that the earth shakes. Since Loki is a god, he always recovers, and he must suffer this fate until the end of the world.

ABOUT THE AUTHOR

John Whitman has written numerous books for young readers, including the Star Wars Galaxy of Fear series and *The Mummy Returns* junior novelization. He lives in California with his family.